LOVE'S ABIDING JOY

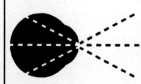

LOVE COMES SOFTLY, BOOK 4

LOVE'S ABIDING JOY

JANETTE OKE

KENNEBEC LARGE PRINT
A part of Gale, Cengage Learning

 GALE
CENGAGE Learning·

Detroit • New York • San Francisco • New Haven, Conn • Waterville, Maine • London

GALE
CENGAGE Learning™

LIBRARY OF CONGRESS CATALOGING-IN-PUBLICATION DATA

Oke, Janette, 1935–
    Love's abiding joy / by Janette Oke.
        p. cm. — (Kennebec Large Print superior collection) (Love
comes softly series ; 4)
    ISBN-13: 978-1-4104-4195-9 (softcover)
    ISBN-10: 1-4104-4195-4 (softcover)
    1. Davis family (Fictitious characters : Oke)—Fiction. 2. Women
pioneers—Fiction. 3. Grandparents—Fiction. 4. Domestic fiction. 5. Large
type books. I. Title.
PR9199.3.O38L57 2011
813'.54—dc22   2011030036

Published in 2011 by arrangement with Bethany House Publishers, a
division of Baker Publishing Group.

Printed in the United States of America
1 2 3 4 5   15 14 13 12 11
ED272

Dedicated with love
to my second sister,
Jean Catherine Budd,
who left us for heaven in 1998,
with deep appreciation for the
many times she was my extra
pair of hands and for her open
heart and open home that always
made me welcome;
and to Orville, the special guy
she brought home to the family, who
was reunited with her in 2001.

CONTENTS

1. Family 9
2. Birthday Dinner 24
3. Planning 32
4. The City 44
5. The Real Journey Begins 60
6. Arrival 87
7. Catching Up 106
8. Marty Meets Maria 125
9. The Rescue 135
10. A Day of a Million Years 160
11. Struggles 182
12. Juan 201
13. Adjustments 218
14. Growing 239
15. Moving 255
16. Winter 269
17. Jedd 283
18. From Death to Life 299

19. Plans and Farewells 315
20. Homeward Bound 328

ONE
FAMILY

"Good mornin'."

The words came softly, and Marty opened sleep-heavy eyes to identify their source. Clark was bending over her, smiling, she noted. Clark did not normally awaken her before his early morning trek to the barn. Marty stirred and stretched, attempting to come fully awake in an effort to understand why he was doing so now.

"Happy birthday."

Oh yes, today was her birthday, and Clark always wanted to be the first one to greet her on her special day. Marty snuggled the covers below her chin, planning to close her eyes again, but she couldn't resist answering his smile.

"An' you woke me jest to remind me thet I'm another year older?" she teased.

"Now, what's wrong with gettin' older? Seems to me it's jest fine — considerin' the alternative," Clark teased back.

Marty smiled again. She was fully awake now. No use trying to get to sleep again.

"Fact is," she said, pushing herself up and reaching to run her hand through Clark's graying hair, "I don't think I'm mindin' this birthday one little bit. I don't feel one speck more'n a day older than I did yesterday. A little short on sleep maybe," she added mischievously, "but not so much older."

Clark laughed. "I've heard tell of people gettin' crotchety and fussy as they age. . . ." He left the sentence hanging but leaned over and took any sting from the words with a kiss on Marty's nose. "Well, I'd best get me to the chorin'. Go ahead, catch yerself a little more shut-eye, iffen ya want to. I'll even git yer breakfast — jest this once."

"Not on yer life," interjected Marty hurriedly. "I'd hafta clean up yer mess in the kitchen." But her hand brushed his cheek, and the love and care between them would have been apparent to anyone who might have been watching.

Clark left, chuckling to himself, and Marty lay back and stretched to her full length beneath the warmth of her handmade quilt. She wouldn't hurry to get up, but Clark's breakfast would be waiting when he returned from the barn.

Today is my birthday, Marty's thoughts

began. Though she wasn't actually feeling older, it seemed, suddenly, that there had been many birthdays. Forty-two, in fact. *Forty-two.* She silently repeated the number in an attempt to grasp the fact of it. *Funny, it really doesn't bother me a bit.* No, there was nothing disturbing about this birthday — not like thirty had been, or forty. My, how she had disliked turning forty! *It seems a body must be near worn out by the time one reaches forty,* she mused. Yet here she was, forty-two, and in all honesty she felt no older than she did when she had come to those previous monumental milestones.

Forty-two, she mulled over the number again but did not dwell on it for long. Instead she thought ahead to the plans for the day. Birthdays meant family. Oh, how she loved to have her family gathered about her! When the children had been little, she herself had been "the maker of birthdays." Now they were grown and old enough that it was her turn to have a special day celebration. Nandry had served the birthday dinner last year, Clae had reminded them at a recent Sunday dinner. Marty couldn't really remember. The years had a tendency to blur together, but, yes, she was sure Clae was right.

Today being Saturday, the birthday dinner

would be held at the noon hour instead of in the evening. Marty liked it better that way. They had so much more time with one another, instead of trying to crowd in the celebration between the return of the schoolchildren and the milking of the cows and other farm chores. Today they would have the whole afternoon ahead of them for visiting and playing with the grandchildren.

Just thinking about the promise of this day filled Marty with anticipation. All thought of sleep now long gone, she threw back the covers, stretched on the edge of the bed, and moved to the window. She looked out upon a beautiful June morning. The world was clean and fresh from last night's rain shower. What a lovely time of year! There was still that lingering feeling of spring in the air, even though many plants had already grown enough to ensure that summer really had arrived. She loved June. Again she felt a stirring of thankfulness to her mother for birthing her in this delightful month.

Marty's thoughts turned to her own children. Nandry . . . Nandry and her little family. The oldest of the Davis brood now had four children of her own, and what a perfect young mother she made. Her husband, Josh, teased about their "baker's dozen," and

Nandry did not even argue with his joking remarks. Yes, their beloved adopted Nandry would have made her natural mama proud. And then there was Nandry's sister, Clae, their second adopted daughter — Clae and her parson husband, Joe. Clae, too, loved children, but Marty felt — though Clae had not said so — that she secretly hoped the size of their family would not grow too quickly. They had one little girl, Esther Sue. Parson Joe still dreamed of getting more seminary training. Marty and Clark added little amounts to the canning jar, which was gradually accumulating funds to help pay for the much-wanted schooling. Marty hoped there would soon be enough for Joe to go, though the thought of their moving so far away was bittersweet.

Marty could feel the smile leave her face and her eyes cloud over as she thought of their next daughter, Missie. Oh, how she missed Missie! She had assumed it was gradually going to get easier over the years of separation, but it had not been so. With every part of her being Marty ached for Missie. *If only . . . if only,* she caught herself thinking again, *if only I could have one chat — if only I could see her again — if only I could hold her children in my arms — if only I could be sure that she is all right, is happy.*

13

But the "if onlys" simply tormented her soul. Marty was here. Missie was many, many days' journey to the west. Yet how she longed for her sweet Missie. Though this daughter was not bone of her bone nor flesh of her flesh — Missie being the daughter of Clark and his first wife, Ellen — Marty felt that Missie was hers in every sense of the word. The tiny motherless baby girl with the pixie face who had stolen her heart and given life special meaning so many years ago was indeed *her* Missie. In fact, Missie had captured her love even before Clark had, she remembered. *Oh, how I miss you, little girl,* Marty whispered against the pane as a tear loosed itself and splashed down on the windowsill. *If only* — But Marty stopped herself with a shake of the head and a lift of her shoulders.

Across the yard she could see Clare and Arnie. Men now in size and years, they each still had much of the little boy in them. Some folks — those not aware of the death of Marty's first husband — were surprised by the differences in their appearance. Clare looked and acted more and more like his father, Clem — big, muscular, teasing, boyish. Arnie was taller, darker, with a sensitive nature and finer features like Clark. By turn they loved each other, teased each other,

14

fought with each other, couldn't live without each other. They were laughing now as they came in for the milk pails, and Clare, who usually did most of the talking, was telling Arnie of some incident at last night's social event. Arnie didn't care much for neighborhood socials, but Clare never missed one. Arnie joined in his brother's laughter at Clare's description of the mishap, but Marty heard him exclaim over and over, "Poor ol' Lou! Poor ol' Lou. I woulda nigh died had it been me." Clare didn't seem to feel any sympathy for "poor ol' Lou," wholeheartedly enjoying the telling of the story. As the boys neared the door, Marty turned away from the window and dressed slowly. There was still lots of time to get the breakfast on. They were just now going to milk.

Marty brushed her long light brown hair and lifted it, heavy and full, to the back of her head. She had sometimes noted the thinning hair on many older women and secretly pitied them. Well, she didn't have any need to worry on that score yet. In fact, her hair had really not shown much gray, either. Not like Clark's. His hair was quite gray at the temples and was even generously sprinkled with gray throughout. *On him it looks good — rather distinguished and manly,*

15

she thought.

Marty dawdled as she pinned up her hair, still examining her thoughts carefully one by one. A birthday was a good time to do some reminiscing. At length, her hair in place, she made up the bed and tidied the room.

As she left the bedroom, the smell of morning coffee wafted up the stairs to her. *Surely Clark didn't carry out his offer to make breakfast* was her first thought. No, she had just seen him down by the far granary. Marty sniffed again. Definitely it was coffee, and fresh-perked, too.

Her curiosity now fully roused, Marty picked up the fragrance of bacon frying and muffins baking. She hurried into the kitchen, her nose fairly twitching with curiosity and the inviting smells.

"Aw, Ma. It was s'posed to be a surprise!"

It was Ellie.

"My land, girl," said Marty, "it sure enough was a surprise, all right! I couldn't figure me out who in the world would be stirrin' 'bout my kitchen this early in the mornin'."

Ellie smiled. "Luke wanted ya to have it in bed. I knew we'd never git thet far without ya knowin', but I thought thet maybe I could have it ready by the time ya

16

came down."

Marty looked at the table. It was covered with a fresh linen cloth and set with the company dishes. A small bowl of wild roses was placed in the center, and each plate and piece of cutlery had been carefully assigned to its place.

"It looks to me like ya are 'bout ready. An' it does look pretty, dear. Those roses look so good I think I could jest sit an' feast my eyes 'stead of my stomach an' not be mindin' it one little bit."

Ellie flushed her pleasure at the praise. "Luke found 'em way over at the other side of the pasture."

Marty buried her nose in the nearest rose, smelling deeply of its fragrance and loving it in a special way because it was given to her in love by a caring family.

"Where is your brother?" she asked when she straightened up.

"Don't think I'm to be tellin' thet," answered Ellie, "but Luke's not far away an' will be back in plenty of time fer breakfast. Ya like a cup of coffee while we're waitin' fer the rest to git here?"

"Thet'd be nice." Marty smiled. Instead of merely a birthday girl, she was beginning to feel like royalty.

Ellie brought Marty's coffee and then

returned to the stove to keep an eye on the breakfast items. Marty sipped slowly, watching her younger daughter over the rim of the cup. Had she realized before just how grown-up Ellie was? Why, she was almost a woman! Any day now she might be taking a notion to cook at her own stove. The thought troubled Marty some. Could she stand to lose another of her girls? The last one? *How lonely to be the only woman in my kitchen!* Ellie had kept life sane and interesting in the years since Missie had left. What would Marty do when Ellie, too, was gone? Why, just the other day, Ma Graham had remarked about what an attractive young woman Ellie had become. Marty, too, had noticed it, but secretly she had been hoping no one else would — not for a while yet. Once people became aware of her little girl turning into a woman and began to whisper, there would be no turning back the clock. Soon their parlor would be buzzing with young gentleman callers, and one of them would be sure to win Ellie's heart. Marty was blinking back some tears when the men came in from the barn.

Clare was first. "Hey, Ma, you don't look so bad, considerin'," he joked, then laughed loudly at his own absurdity as though it were something truly hilarious.

Arnie looked embarrassed. "Aw, Clare, nothin' funny 'bout yer dumb —"

But Clare slapped him noisily on the back and declared with good humor, "Ma, ya forgot to have 'em give this kid of yers a funny bone when they made him up. Don't know how to laugh, this kid."

Clare then turned his attention to his sister. "Hey, it still smells all right. Haven't ya got it to the burnin' stage yet?"

Ellie laughed and tried to swipe a wet dishrag across his face, but he ducked away. She was used to Clare's teasing. Besides, she doted on her oldest brother, and he would have done anything in the world for her. Clare roughed her hair and went to wash for breakfast. Ellie tried to pat her hair back into its proper place, then dished up the scrambled eggs. Arnie, content to wait his turn at the washbasin, finally crossed to Marty. "Happy birthday, Ma," he said, laying his hand on her shoulder.

"Thank ya, son. It sure has had a promisin' start."

"An' soon we'll all be headin' for Clae's. Boy, those kids of Nandry's git noisier ever' time we see 'em. 'Uncle Arnie, give me a ride.' 'Uncle Arnie, lift me up.' 'Uncle Arnie, help me.' 'Uncle Arnie —' "

"An' you love every minute of it," cut in Ellie.

Arnie did not argue, only grinned. Marty nodded her agreement with Ellie. Arnie did indeed love the kids.

Clark came in, drying his hands on a towel, and glanced around the kitchen. "Well, it 'pears thet my family has 'bout gathered in. Everyone waitin' on me?"

"Yeah, thought you'd never git here, Pa," said Clare, taking the rough farm towel and winding it up to snap at Arnie.

"The boys jest now came in," Ellie informed her pa, "so I guess you haven't kept anyone waitin' any."

The men, finished with their washing and fooling around, took their places at the table. Marty moved her chair into position, and Ellie brought the platter of hot bacon from the stove. Marty looked at the empty place. "Luke," she said. "Luke isn't here yet."

"Still sleepin'?" asked Clare, knowing that Luke did enjoy a good sleep-in on occasion.

"He'll be here in a minute," said Ellie. "I think he'd like fer us to jest go ahead."

"But —" Marty protested, and just then the screen door banged and in came Luke, his hair disheveled by the wind and his face flushed from hurrying. Marty's heart gave a

20

skip at the sight of her "baby." Luke was her gentle one, her peacemaker and dream-builder. Luke, fifteen, was smaller than the other boys and had serious and caring soft brown eyes. Marty felt she had never seen another person whose eyes looked as warm and compassionate as her little Luke's.

"Sorry," he said under his breath and slid into his place at the table.

Clark's love for the boy showed in his simple nod. "Would you like to wash?"

"I can wait until we pray; then the food won't be gittin' cold."

"Reckon the food will wait well enough. Go ahead."

Luke hurried from the table, inspecting his hands as he went. They were covered with red stains. He was soon back, and the family sat quietly as Clark read the morning Scripture portion and then led in prayer.

His prayer of the morning included a special thanks for the mother of the home and his helpmate over the years. Clark reminded the Lord that Marty was truly worthy of His special blessing. Marty re-membered an earlier prayer, so long ago when she was a hurting, bewildered, and reluctant bride. Clark had asked the Father to bless her then, too. God had. She had felt Him with her through the years, and these dear children about her table were evidence of His blessing.

After the prayer ended and the food was passed, Clare looked over at Luke between bites of bacon and eggs. "So, little brother. What ya been up to so early in the mornin'?"

Luke squirmed a bit. "Well, I jest wanted Ma to have some strawberries fer her birthday breakfast, but boy — were they little and hard to find this year! Guess it ain't been warm enough yet." He held out a small cup of tiny strawberries.

Marty's throat constricted and her eyes filled again with tears. Her sleepyhead had crawled out early to get her some birthday strawberries. She remembered back to when Missie had first started the tradition of "strawberries for Ma's birthday breakfast." After Missie had left, the children had pooled their efforts for a few years. Then with the breaking of the pastureland that had housed the best strawberry patch, the tradition had drifted away. And now dear Luke had tried valiantly to revive it again.

Clare reached over and roughed his younger brother's hair. His eyes said, *You're all right, ya know that, kid,* but his mouth was too busy with Ellie's breakfast muffins.

"Ya should have told me," Arnie whispered. "I'da helped ya."

Marty looked around the kitchen at the four children still sharing their table, and her heart filled with joy and overflowed with love. The smile she shared with Clark needed no words of explanation.

Two
Birthday Dinner

"Thet was a lovely dinner, Clae," Marty remarked, delicately catching the last traces of cake crumbs from her lips with the tip of her tongue. Clare's satisfied groan as he held his full stomach was eloquent. Nandry's Josh laughed.

As the plates were pushed back and another round of coffee poured, the pleasant clamor of visiting began. It seemed that everyone had something to say all at once, including the children. Clark held up his hands for silence and eventually drew the attention of even the youngest in the group.

"Hold it," he chuckled, "ain't nobody gonna hear nobody in all this racket. How 'bout a little organization here?"

Nandry's oldest, Tina, giggled. "Oh, Grandpa, how can one org'nize chatter?"

"Can I go now? Can I go play with Uncle Arnie?" Andrew interrupted, the only boy in Nandry and Josh's family.

"Just before we all leave the table and scatter who knows where, how about if we let Grandma open up her birthday gifts?" suggested Clae.

"Oh yes! Let's. Let's!" shouted the children, clapping their hands. Presents were always fun, even if they were for someone else.

Grandma Marty was given the chair of honor, and the gifts began to arrive, carried in and presented by various family members. The children shared scraps of artwork and pictures. Tina had even hemmed, by hand stitch, a new handkerchief. Nandry and Clae, presenting gifts from their families, laughed when they realized they had both sewn Marty new aprons. Clare and Arnie had gone together and purchased a brand-new teapot, declaring that now she could "git rid of thet ol' one with the broken spout." *Not too likely* was Marty's silent comment. *I'll plant spring flowers in it and put it in the kitchen window.* But aloud she admired the fancy new one.

Ellie's gift to her mother was a delicate cameo brooch, and Marty suspected that Clark had contributed largely to its purchase. Luke was last. His eyes showed both eagerness and embarrassment as he came slowly forward. It was clear he was just a bit

25

uncertain as to how the others would view his gift.

"I'm afraid it didn't cost nothin'," he murmured.

"Thet isn't what gives a gift its value," Marty replied, both curious and concerned.

"I know you always said thet, but some folk . . . well . . . they think thet ya shouldn't give what cost ya nothin'."

"Ah," said Clark, seeming to realize what was bothering the boy, "but the cost is not always figured in dollars and cents. To give of yerself sometimes be far more costly than reachin' into one's pocket fer cash."

Luke smiled and looked more at ease as he pushed a clumsy package toward Marty.

"Ya said thet ya liked 'em, so . . ." He shrugged and backed away as his mother reached for the gift.

Heavy and bulky, it was wrapped in brown paper and tied at the top with store twine. Marty was trying to imagine what kind of a gift could come in such a package. She untied the twine with hurried fingers and let the brown paper fall stiffly to the floor. Before her eyes lay two small shrubs, complete with roots and part of the countryside in which they had grown. Marty recognized them at once as small bushes from the hill country. One summer when she and Clark had taken the youngsters into the hills for a family outing, she had exclaimed over them when in full bloom. How beautiful they had looked in their dress of scarlet blossoms. She caught her breath as she visualized the beautiful shrubs blooming in her own garden.

"Do you think they'll grow okay, Pa?" Luke's anxiety was clear in his voice. "I tried to be as careful as I could in diggin' 'em up. Tried to be sure to keep from hurtin' the roots an' —"

"We'll give 'em the best possible care an' try to match their home-growin' conditions as much as possible," Clark assured Luke, then continued under his breath, "— iffen I have to haul their native soil from them hills by the wagonload."

Marty couldn't stop the tears this time. It was so much like Luke. He had traveled many miles and had gone to a great deal of effort and care in order to present to her the shrubs he knew she loved. And yet he had stood in embarrassment before his family, his eyes begging them to please try to understand his gift and the reason for his giving it. She pulled him gently to her and hugged him close. Luke wasn't too fond of motherly kisses in public places, so Marty refrained from any further attention.

"Thank you, son," she said quietly. "I can hardly wait fer them to bloom."

Luke grinned and moved back into the family circle.

All eyes then turned to Clark. It had become a family tradition that the final gift to be given at such family gatherings was always from the head of the home. Clark cleared his throat now and stood to his feet.

"Well, my gift ain't as pretty as some thet sit here. It'll never bloom in years to come, either. But it does come with love, an' I hope it be somethin' thet truly gives ya pleasure. No fancy package — jest this here little envelope."

He handed the plain brown envelope to Marty. She turned it over in her hand, looking for some writing that would indicate what she was holding. There was nothing.

"Open it, Gram'ma," came a small voice, quickly echoed by many others.

Marty carefully tore off one corner, slit the envelope open, and let the contents fall into her lap — two pieces of paper and on them words in Clark's handwriting. Marty picked up the first. Aloud she read the message. "This is for the new things that you be needing. Just let me know when and where you want to do the shopping."

"Ya should have read the other one first,"

28

interjected Clark.

Marty picked up the second slip of paper and read, "Arrangements have been made for tickets on the train to Missie. We leave —"

Tickets to go to Missie! All Marty's recent thoughts and longings centering on their daughter so many miles away, all those "if onlys" crowded in around her. She was going to see Missie again. "Oh, Clark!" was all she could manage, and then she was in his arms sobbing for the wonder of it — the pure joy of the promise the tickets held.

When she finally could control herself, she stepped back from Clark's embrace. With a joyful heart but trembling lips, Marty said apologetically to her family, "I think I need me a little walkin' time, an' then we're gonna sit us down an' talk all 'bout this. . . ." She did well to get that far without more tears, and she left the cozy kitchen filled with the family she loved and walked out into the June sunshine.

Here at Clae's there was no place in particular to go, so she simply wandered aimlessly around the yard. The familiar trees and little spring behind her own house had been her refuge many times over the years when she had some thinking to do. Well, Clae's trees would suffice, she told herself.

She tried to collect her scattered, excited thoughts. She was going to see Missie! She and Clark would travel those many miles on the train. No wagons — no slow days of wind and rain. Only padded seats and chugging engines eating up the distance between her little girl and herself. Oh, she could hardly wait! She held up the note she still clutched in her hand and read it aloud again. *"Arrangements have been made for tickets on the train to Missie. We leave as soon as you can be ready to go. Love, Clark."*

As soon as you can be ready to go. Oh my. There was so much to be done. So many things to prepare and take with them. There was her wardrobe. She would need new things for traveling. Why, her blue hat would never do to wear out among stylish people, and her best dress had a small snag near the hem that still showed even though she had mended it carefully. *Oh my.* How would she ever — ? And then Marty remembered the second note. *This is for the new things that you be needing. Just let me know when and where you want to do the shopping.*

"Oh my," Marty said aloud. Clark had thought of everything, it appeared. "Oh my," she repeated and quickly changed direction back to Clae's kitchen. She must talk to the girls. They were far more aware of the present fashion trends, and they knew what stores carried the needed articles, and they knew where she should go to do her shopping and when the stages ran between the towns. "Oh my," she said again in a flurry, "I do have me so much to do. Oh my."

THREE
PLANNING

The days that followed were full of excited thinking and planning. Nandry and Clae went shopping with Marty for yard goods in their small town and then pored over design sketches that Clae made in an effort to achieve fashionable gowns. It was finally concluded that a trip to a larger center would be necessary if Marty was to be presentable to the outside world on a cross-country train trip. But when could she work that outing in to this busy time? Though her wardrobe consumed much of Marty's time and attention, there were other matters that weighed heavily on her mind, as well. One of them was the fact that Clare had wedding plans. As yet, a definite date for the marriage had not been set, but how could they go way off west not knowing? Marty held her tongue, but she did try to "plant the seed" in Clare's thinking that it would be most helpful if he and his young lady could finalize a date. Clare understood the subtle suggestion and told Marty he would see what he could do.

Marty was also anxious about the packing. It wasn't her own things that gave her worries, but every day she thought of something new that surely Missie and Willie and their young family might need. How much dare she accumulate before the railroad company — or Clark — would declare she had far too much baggage? She sighed as she tried to sort and select the most important items.

Clark occasionally tried to draw out an estimated day for departure from Marty. She knew a decision must be made. Clark had many responsibilities of his own that needed to be assigned to others. He couldn't properly sort them out until Marty had given him some idea as to when she would be ready to go. She didn't know whether to hope that Clare would set the wedding date for the immediate future or postpone it until they were sure to be back.

Then, of course, there were the other children. True, Ellie was capable of caring for the household, but it seemed like a big job to put on such young, slender shoulders. Marty conveniently forgot that at Ellie's age she had already been a married woman.

Yet Marty's heart was most concerned for Luke, her gentle youngest. How she wished they could take him with them. At the same time, she was afraid to suggest it, even to Clark. What if Luke did go, and what if he decided that he liked Missie's West, and what if he decided not to come back when Clark and Marty returned home? No, she'd best leave Luke safely where he was. She had no desire to have another child settled so far away from home.

So Marty spent her days musing and fretting. She tried not to let it show, but it must have. Nandry and Clae made arrangements for the care of their children and planned a trip to the city by local stagecoach for shopping. Ellie was invited to go along. With their loving but firm counsel, the necessary items were decided on, purchased, and prepared for travel. Marty was afraid she was spending an inappropriate amount of money, but she did rather enjoy this unusual extravagance. She also bought a few pretty things to take to Missie, as well. Who knew whether Missie had opportunity to shop since leaving her home?

Clare discussed marriage plans with his sweet Kate and, with the help of her mother, they were able to arrive at a suitable date. They wisely agreed that a hurried wedding would not be a good start for their marriage, so August 27 was chosen. Clark and Marty would have no problem being home by then. Clare and Kate planned to live in Clark's first little log home, so Clare would spend the intervening time preparing the place for occupancy, and Kate would spend her time on new curtains and floor rugs.

Ellie asked many questions and advice on the running of the home and the tending of the garden — questions to which she already knew the answers, but she probably knew it would help her mother depart with greater peace of mind if she explained it all again. Ellie assured Marty that she was looking forward to the experience, and Marty felt that it might truly be an adventure for the girl. Nandry and Clae promised to lend a hand if ever she needed assistance.

Luke took to making subtle observations about the coming separation. He suggested that it would be good for all of them to spend some time on their own and learn some independence. He pointed out to Marty that he would be spending most evenings studying for the entrance exams for college the coming fall, and he would have very little time for socializing even with family members. The additional quiet of the house during their absence would be very helpful in giving him extra study time, he said. Marty sensed he was trying to put her mind at ease about going off and leaving him, and she appreciated his concern.

Many times a day Marty went through the process of mentally sorting what she wished to take. She eyed her garden, her canned goods, her sewing materials, her chicken coop — she even eyed the milk cows. She shook her head. How in the world would she ever decide? At length, she knew she could never be sensible, so she asked for help from her family in the final decisions. Eventually it was narrowed down to a list over which Clark did not ruefully shake his head.

At length Clark was given the go-ahead. He could set a date for departure. It seemed that within a few more days, Marty could be ready to go.

"When are ya leavin'?" asked Ma Graham when they had a minute together after the church service.

Marty was relieved that she actually had a date. "Well, we take the stage out from town on Wednesday, and go on over to catch the train out of the city the next mornin'," she replied.

"Ain't ya excited?" Ma asked, but didn't need nor wait for an answer. "My, I miss thet girl of yourn so much myself thet I can jest imagine how yer feelin'. Give Missie a big kiss an' hug fer me. I have a little some-thin' here thet I want ya to take on out to her. I didn't dare send nothin' big — ya havin' so much of yer own stuff to tend to, so I jest made her a little lace doily fer her table."

Marty hugged Ma warmly, the tears in her eyes.

"Missie will 'preciate it so much," she whispered in a choked voice.

And so the packing of the crates, cases, and trunk was finished up, the clothes for travel carefully laid out, and the scattered items and thoughts collected. Many last-minute instructions, some necessary and some only for Marty's sake, were given to the three boys and Ellie. There was some measure of assurance in just reviewing them over and over.

Clare and Arnie had been farming right along with Clark for a number of years, so Clark had no doubts about their ability to take care of things. They each had a piece of their own land to farm now, too, but they could handle it all in Clark's absence. They had been instructed to get help if ever they needed it, and Luke was anxious to provide all the help his studying time would allow.

Without it actually being discussed, everyone understood that Luke probably would never be a farmer. He had a very keen mind and a sensitive spirit and was presently leaning toward the possibility of being a medical doctor. Clark and Marty felt he would be a great honor to them as a doctor, but Luke was not pressured for a commitment on his future.

And so the farming was left to the boys and the kitchen to Ellie. Marty knew she was quite able to care for the needs of the brothers, but still Marty fretted some as she thought of all the work ahead for the young girl.

The day of their departure dawned clear and bright, and the warm sunshine spilled through the bedroom window. Marty was up even before Clark and, in her excitement, flitted about working on last-minute things that really needed no attention. Her efforts were not totally without value, for it did give her something to do until it was time for them to load into the spring-seated wagon and head for town.

The four children from home accompanied them, and when they arrived — too early — at the stagecoach offices, Nandry and Josh and their family, and Clae and Joe and Esther Sue were already there.

The excitement was felt by everyone and resulted in too many talking at once, too much nervous activity, and too many near-wild children. Clark grinned around at the whole tension-filled bunch of them.

"Whoa," he finally called, lifting up his hand, his signal for quiet. "How 'bout we see iffen we can git a little order out of this confusion?" Everyone stopped midsentence and midstep and then began to laugh.

"I suggest," went on Clark, "thet we go on over to the hotel an' have us a cup of coffee an' a sandwich. Be a heap quieter, an' we still have lots of time to kill before this here stage is gonna be leavin'." Eventually they all fell into line and headed for the hotel and the promised coffee. Josh broke line, whispered to Nandry, and then fished in his pocket.

"Tina, yer ma says it be okay fer ya to take these here little ones over to the general store fer a candy treat. It being a special day, how 'bout ya all git *two* pieces of yer favorite kind."

Shouts of approval answered him, and he passed Tina the coins. She took Mary and Esther Sue by the hands and headed for the promised treat. Andrew disdained holding hands and marched off on his own. Baby Jane was content to be held in her mother's arms and to put up with the grown-ups while they visited over coffee cups.

When they finally were seated and had placed their orders, the talking did become a bit more orderly. They even waited for one another to finish their sentences before breaking in with a new thought or question. Marty knew her churning stomach had no interest in a sandwich. She ordered a cup of tea and sipped at it now and then between the talk and laughter. The men ordered sandwiches and even pieces of pie to go with them. Marty wondered fleetingly how they ever managed it, only a few hours since they had downed a big breakfast.

Departure time seemed to be in no hurry to come. The food had been eaten, the cups drained, replenished, and drained again, the same admonitions given and repeated, and the same assurances spoken over and over. Marty fidgeted in her seat. Clark at last said he supposed they could go on out and check on the progress of the stagecoach.

As they stood chatting before the stagecoach office, Zeke LaHaye, Willie's pa, joined them. He greeted them all with one nod and sweep of his hat, then reached to shake Clark's hand.

"Guess I needn't tell ya how I envy you. Sure would love to head on out with ya.

Always had me a hankerin' to see the west country, an' with my boy out there it sure does git awfully hard to jest hold myself here at home sometimes."

"Well, now," said Clark, "ya oughta throw in yer bedroll an' come along."

Zeke answered with a smile. "Sure is temptin'. Did bring this here little parcel if-fen ya think ya can find a little room fer it someplace. Hate to be botherin' ya like, but it jest ain't possible to let ya go without send-in' somethin' along fer the family."

"No trouble. No trouble a'tall," assured Clark and placed the parcel with the stack of their belongings.

Marty looked at the big pile of things go-ing west. There were all of their own daily necessities, the many things they had packed to take to Willie and Missie, the added articles from Clae and Nandry, the gifts from Ma Graham, Wanda Marshall, Sally Anne, and even some from Missie's students during her teaching days. Yes, the pile had grown and grown and, indeed, each ad-ditional item meant "more trouble," but she would have no more denied Zeke LaHaye the pleasure of sending something to his family than she would have denied herself. She'd discard her new hatbox if necessary in order to make room.

The stage finally appeared, two minutes early, and all the baggage and crates were loaded. Zeke's package fit in, too, and Marty was able to tuck in the hatbox.

Over and over the words, "Ya tell Willie . . ." or "Give Missie . . ." or "Kiss them for me," were echoed from family members. Marty turned to each one with tears in her eyes and pounding heart. It was so exciting to finally be on their way. If only "good-byes" didn't need to come before one had the pleasure of "hellos." She kissed Luke one last time, gave Ellie one more hug, threw kisses to the many-times-kissed grandchildren, and hurried forward lest the stage driver get impatient with her.

The good-bye shouts followed them on down the road. Marty leaned from the window for one last wave before the coach turned the corner, and then she settled back against the already warm seat.

"I do declare," she remarked seriously to Clark, "I do believe thet travelin' be awful hard work. I feel all worn out like."

"We've barely started travelin', Marty," Clark laughed softly. "It's not the travelin' thet has ya all tuckered. It's the gettin' ready and the excitement. From now on, ya have nothin' to do but jest rest."

Marty smiled at Clark's calm assessment

but felt rather doubtful. How could she ever rest when her whole body vibrated with excited energy? Well, she'd try. She'd try.

FOUR
THE CITY

An awfully long, dusty, warm stagecoach trip faced Clark and Marty on the first leg of their journey. At least in their own farm wagon, they could catch the breezes and stop occasionally to stretch their legs. The morning sun moved up high in the sky, beating down unmercifully, and the open windows helped only a little. The other three passengers were men. Clark talked to them some, but Marty found little of interest in the conversation. Besides, her mind was on many other things. Had she brought the things that Missie really could use? How big was little Nathan now, the grandson they had never seen?

In spite of the warmth in the stagecoach, Marty knew that a stylish traveling lady did not remove her hat, even in the heat of the day, but how she longed to lift hers from her warm head and let it lie in her lap.

They stopped to change horses and to allow the passengers a few moments to walk around. Marty was enormously grateful for the bit of respite. Then on they went again, bumping over the rough tracks of the road. Marty had assumed the road would be fairly well traveled and smooth, but the stage wheels seemed to find every rut available.

At noon another rest stop was taken, and Marty climbed stiffly down with Clark's assistance and sought out the shade of some nearby trees. The men scattered in various directions to walk, sit, or stretch out on the cool grass.

Marty took their little lunch bag and spread out a noonday meal of sandwiches and cool drink with tarts and cookies for dessert. Marty herself wasn't much interested, but she noted that the traveling was not adversely affecting Clark's appetite.

All too soon the stage was ready to move on again. They left the coolness of the trees and took their places on the hot, dusty leather seats. The minutes of the afternoon ticked away with the grinding and bumping of the wheels and the steady rhythm of the horses' hooves. Occasionally, a hoot or shout from the driver would call some new order to the teams.

In spite of the heat and discomfort, Marty found her head nodding. Probably the fact that she had been missing some sleep in recent days helped to make her drowsy. But it was hard to actually sleep in the jostling wagon. As soon as she would find herself slipping into relaxing slumber, another bump or shake would snap her awake. She found it to be worse than no sleep at all. She shifted position and fought to remain awake, catching glimpses of countryside through the stage windows.

A change of teams at another stagecoach station broke up the monotony of the afternoon. Marty's back and legs ached, and she was thankful for the stretch. She thought of Missie's long journey west by wagon train and more fully appreciated their courage through the discomfort of it all.

It was almost suppertime when the stagecoach pulled into the city station. Marty leaned forward eagerly to see all that she could as they traveled the busy, crowded streets, then realized she probably looked like a country bumpkin. She settled back against the seat and allowed only her eyes to move from side to side at a world very different from her own.

After alighting, Marty walked around, flexing her muscles and observing all of the strange sights and sounds as Clark collected their belongings and made the proper arrangements for everything to be on the morning's train west. All they took with them for the immediate were two cases and Marty's hatbox. Marty felt a bit panicky as she watched their luggage being carted away. Was the man truly dependable? Would he be *sure* to put them on the right train? Would everything arrive safely? Was it all properly labeled? What would they ever do if it did not make it?

But Clark seemed to have no such worries. Seemingly relieved and confident that he had all things arranged in good order, he took her arm.

"Well, Mrs. Davis," he teased, "here we are in the big city. What shall we be doin' with it?"

"Doin'?" asked Marty blankly.

"Well, they say a big city is full of all manner of excitin' an' forbidden things. Ya be wishin' to go lookin' fer some of 'em?"

Marty no doubt looked as shocked as she felt. "Me?"

Clark laughed. "No, not you. An' not me, either. I'm jest funnin' ya. I have heard they have some very good eatin' places, though. I could sure use me some good food. Somethin' about sandwiches thet don't stay with a man fer long. Though they sure enough hit the spot at the time, ya understand." He chuckled again as he looked into her face. "Ya interested?"

"I reckon," replied Marty, though secretly she found herself far more interested in what the people would be wearing than in what they ate.

"Well, let's jest find us a hotel room to git settled an' leave our belongin's, an' then we'll see what we be findin'."

They discovered a hotel quickly enough. It was the largest one Marty had ever seen. She looked around the lobby at the high ornate ceiling, the glistening hanging lights, and the elaborately paneled doors. *This is going to cost us nigh onto a fortune,* she thought, but she did not voice her opinion to Clark.

Clark was handed a key and given a few instructions, and then he gathered up their bags and took Marty's arm for the climb up the stairs — many of them. But she soon was distracted by the attractive paper on the walls and the colorful carpeting beneath their feet. At length, Clark stopped before a door and used the key. He pushed the door open and then stood to the side to allow Marty to enter. The room before them was the most elegant Marty had ever seen. She looked about her, studying carefully every detail. She wanted to be able to describe the room to her daughters.

The wallpaper was a richly patterned blue and the draperies were deep blue velvet with thick fringes. The bedspread, heavy and brocaded, had a cream background with some blue threads interwoven. The ornate chest appeared to have been hand-carved, and there was a special stool or small table on which one rested the travel cases. The imported carpet was a riot of rich purples, crimsons, blues, and golds, all blended together in an attractive overall pattern. The room even had its own bathroom. Marty took it all in and then turned to Clark.

"My," she said, then again, "my, I never know'd thet all of this grandness was possible."

"I jest hope thet this 'grandness' has a comfortable bed," he responded dryly, crossing over to the bed and testing it with his hand. "I'm thinkin' thet before mornin' I'll likely be pinin' fer the 'grandness' of our own four-poster."

Marty, too, felt the bed. "Feels fine to me," she stated, "though I admit to feelin' so tired thet a plank floor might even be welcome."

Clark laughed. "Before ya settle fer thet plank floor, let's go see what this here town has to offer an empty stomach." And, so saying, he attempted to lead her from the room.

"Whoa now," argued Marty. "Iffen I'm gonna dine out like a fine lady, I'm gonna need to freshen up first. Goodness sakes, the stage was so hot an' dusty, one feels in fair need of a bath an' hairwash."

As expected, it took Marty longer to prepare for going out than it did Clark. He waited fairly patiently while she primped and fussed and finally felt confident enough to venture forth. They descended the stairs slowly, and Clark made inquiry as to the location of a nice dining room. Assured that the one in the hotel was one of the finest the city had to offer, they proceeded into an immense room with elaborate columns and deep wine-colored draperies. Marty had never dined in such splendor. She could scarcely take her eyes from the room and its occupants long enough to properly select from the menu. Everything on the stiff card before her looked too fussy, too much, and too expensive. It was hard for her to make up her mind. She wished she could find something simple like fried chicken or roast beef. Clark asked for the house specialty and, without checking to see what it was, Marty echoed his order.

She tried not to stare, but the people moving about the room and sitting at the white-covered tables seemed to be from another world. She had to take herself consciously in hand and remember her manners. Still, she was relieved and pleased to note that she did not stand out in the crowd as "backwoods" or "frumpish." Her daughters had chosen her new clothing well. How thankful she was for their knowledge and encouragements.

When the waiters had brought their plates and settled the dishes in front of them, Clark took Marty's hand and bowed his head, thanking the Lord for His care on the journey and for the food before them. The meal was delicious, though they served far too large a portion in Marty's opinion. She, who was not in the habit of wasting anything, had a difficult time leaving the food on her plate and sending it back to the kitchen. She was concerned, too, that the cook might take offense and feel that the meal had not pleased her. After she had eaten all she possibly could and pushed back her plate, she still was not sure exactly what she had eaten. It had been very tasty — but not identifiable like her home-cooked farm suppers of roast beef, potatoes, and gravy. Everything about the city was different.

They ordered French pastries to go with their coffee and lingered over them, enjoying the taste, the atmosphere, and the pleasurable luxury of sitting with no responsibility to hasten them away from the table.

When they felt it would be impolite to remain any longer, they rose from the table and returned to the lobby. Clark purchased a local paper and tucked it under his arm as they again made their way up the stairs to their room. Marty held her skirt carefully as she climbed; it would never do to step clumsily on her skirt and damage such an expensive hemline.

"So how do you plan on spendin' this lazy evenin', with no mendin' or sewin' in yer hands?" Clark asked as he opened the door to their room.

"Isn't botherin' me none," responded Marty lightly. "As tired as I be feelin', I expect thet sleep sounds 'bout as good to me as anythin' I could be doin'."

Clark smiled. "Go on. Tuck yerself in then. Me, I'm jest gonna check the paper an' see what's goin' on in the world."

Marty prepared for bed and slipped between the cool, smooth sheets with a contented sigh. Oh, how tired she was! She longed for a good long sleep. She would be off before you could say . . . But it turned out she wasn't. Try as she might to relax in the big soft bed, her mind still kept whirling. She thought of Missie and her little family they were going to see. She thought of Ellie, Luke, Arnie, and Clare back home. Was there anything she had forgotten to tell them, any reminders she hadn't given, any instructions she had missed? Would their baggage really make it onto the train? What would it be like sharing the close proximity of a train car with strangers for days on end as they traveled? Marty's mind buzzed with questions.

Clark finished reading his paper, prepared for retiring, and climbed in beside her. Soon Marty heard his soft breathing and knew he slept in spite of the unfamiliar bed. Still sleep eluded her. She stirred restlessly and wished for morning. Once they were actually on that train and headed for Missie's, she was sure *then* she could relax.

In spite of her restless night, Marty roused herself early the next morning. Anticipation took charge, driving her from the bed. Clark stirred as Marty threw back the blankets.

"Rooster crow already?" he teased, then shut his eyes again and turned over.

Marty didn't let his joshing bother her but went about her morning preparations. She had already decided on the dress and hat she would wear for their first train ride and carefully worked out the wrinkles with the palms of her hands. She shook out the hat, fluffing up the feather, and stepped back to admire the plume. *My, this is some hat,* she thought. She felt a mite self-conscious about wearing it, but then assured herself that all the fashionable traveling ladies wore them.

Marty dressed carefully and then began packing her nightclothes and her gown of yesterday in her case. The gown smelled dusty and looked bedraggled from the stagecoach ride. *What a shame to pack it away in such a mess!* she fretted. She wished there were some way to freshen it first. She selected a few pages from Clark's newspaper and carefully wrapped the dress in it. Clark, still in bed, seemed not the least disturbed by the crackling newspaper.

Marty finished all her packing and preparation for their second day of travel, and Clark still hadn't stirred. She wasn't sure what she should do. She hated to waken him, but what if they were late and missed their train? She had no idea of the time. She crossed to where Clark's vest hung on the back of a chair and fumbled in his breast pocket for his pocket watch. *It isn't there!* Marty panicked and her mind immediately flashed to the terrible stories she had heard about the big city. They were true! Someone must have come into their room in the dead of night and stolen Clark's watch. If his watch was gone, what else had they taken? Marty hurried to her case. Was her cameo from Ellie still there? And what about the gold brooch that Clark had given her two Christmases ago?

Marty had packed them on the very bottom of the suitcase. Carefully now she lifted each item from the case, going down on her knees on the floor to lay things out all around her. When she remembered the hours she had spent carefully packing each item of her clothing, she could have cried. Would she ever get them so neatly arranged again? Many of the gowns she had folded in thin tissue wrap supplied by the dress shops in which she had made her purchases. And now, as she lifted them out, no matter how hard she tried to be careful, she disturbed the garments and wrinkled the tissue. Yet she *had* to know — were her few items of precious jewelry stolen along with Clark's watch? Clark would be so disappointed! His three sons had gone together to purchase the gift for his last birthday, and he had proudly worn the watch chain across his chest.

Marty stopped suddenly in the middle of her frantic search. Perhaps she shouldn't be wasting precious time now. Perhaps she should run down to the front desk and report the loss. Maybe there still was a chance to catch the thief. No, first she must know how many missing things to report. So Marty continued unpacking her case, item by item, laying each one around her in one of the neat piles on the deep blues, golds, wines, and scarlets of the carpeted floor.

Marty was almost to the last item when Clark roused from sleep and sat up in bed.

"Ya repackin'?" Clark asked mildly, though his expression looked rather dumb-founded.

"Oh, Clark!" Marty cried. "I'm so glad yer finally awake. We've had us thieves in the night." Marty's hands hurried on, emptying the last few items from her case.

"Thieves?"

"Yes, indeed."

"What ya meanin', *thieves*?"

But Marty interrupted him with a glad cry. "Oh, they're still here! Oh, I'm so glad, so glad."

Clark was out of bed by then, looking down at Marty, who clasped her precious jewelry to her bosom.

"Look!" she cried. "They didn't find 'em."

"Who find what? I'm not followin' —"

"The thieves — the thieves who stole yer watch. Oh, Clark, I'm so sorry. I know how much ya loved thet watch an' —"

"Ya meanin' this watch?" Clark asked, lifting it from the small table by the bed.

Marty gasped, "Ya found it!"

"Found it? I never lost it. I put it there by my bed so's I could check the time in the mornin'."

"Oh, Clark. I checked in yer pockets fer it, an' when I couldn't find it I thought thet someone had —"

But Clark had started to laugh. He pointed at Marty and at the empty case and the heaped-up clothing and laughed uproariously.

At first Marty felt chagrined by his outburst, since she was not yet over her concern and fear during the trying ordeal of the last several minutes. Then she looked about her at the clutter and then at the watch held dangling from its chain in Clark's hand, and the humor of the situation struck her also. She buried her face in her hands and laughed with Clark.

When she finally had control of herself again, she gasped out, "Well, if this isn't 'bout the dumbest thing I've ever done. Jest look at me! I think thet my sleepless nights have really addled my brain. Oh, Clark, jest look at the mess I got here!"

Then a new thought struck her. The repacking of the case was going to take some time if she was going to do it carefully. Perhaps she would need to stuff things into the case and run to catch the train. Nervously, she looked up, her hands quickly starting to return things to their proper places. "How much time we got 'fore — ?"

Clark assured her they had far more time than she would ever need for the repacking, even though she was "as particular and fussy as Aunt Gertie." Marty had never come by any more information than that about Aunt Gertie, but when Clark wanted to make a point of someone's fussiness, he always brought up this aunt of his. The boys had taken up the phrase, too, though they knew nothing more than she did of the mysterious Aunt Gertie.

Marty, relieved that there was plenty of time, carefully set out to put everything back in its proper place while Clark shaved and dressed.

She was still laboring over the open case when Clark stood, hat in hand, ready to go.

"Be it time?" Marty inquired.

"Take yer time — we still got lots of it.

Soon as yer ready, we'll go on down an' find us some breakfast. A man can't travel on an empty stomach. Then we'll come back on up an' pick up our things." Clark tipped up Marty's chin and looked into her face with a smile. "Guess we might as well do the rest of our waitin' at the train station. I have me a feelin' thet yer not gonna rest easy until yer sure thet yer gonna be on thet there train," he added.

Marty packed in the last few items and closed the case. She stood to her feet and nodded her head. There was no use denying what Clark had just said. He knew her far too well.

"I'm ready now," she said. "An', yes, I could be usin' some breakfast."

Clark offered his arm, checked his safe-in-hand watch, shook his head a bit, and chuckled again.

Five
The Real Journey Begins

At the train station, Marty was sure she had never seen so many people all in one place. Her eyes and ears were busy noting and storing up the new sights and sounds all around her. *What would Nandry, Clae, and Ellie think if they could see all this!*

Clark found a bench on which Marty could wait and went to make final arrangements for their journey. She sat and watched the array of marvelously colorful dresses, even on little girls. Why, the menfolk looked like they belonged on the pages of some storybook!

Even though there was still lots of time before the train was due to leave the station, Clark had been correct about her state of mind. Marty would not really rest easy until she was actually seated on the train and assured that its engine was pulling them westward. So in spite of her interest in the crowd, she fidgeted and was glad when she saw Clark moving back across the room toward her.

A rather confident looking woman with bright hair and a broad-brimmed scarlet-plumed hat sat across the room. To Marty's surprise, the woman also seemed to be watching Clark's approach. The woman looked out from under her hat brim, then she seemed to deliberately drop a glove at her own feet and pretended to go back to the book she held before her face. As Clark reached the "lost" glove, he bent, gentlemanlike, recovered it, and then glanced around to see who its owner might be. Marty saw the woman steal a very small peek, and then her long eyelashes began to flutter. Marty knew she was about to make her presence known to Clark in some clever little speech.

Marty stood quickly and spoke before the lady in the hat had time to open her mouth. "Everythin' set, Clark? Oh, a glove. Perhaps it belongs to you, ma'am," she said, reaching for it and turning to the woman with a smile. "It matches your hat perfectly."

The lady accepted her glove without comment. Marty moved away, taking Clark's arm and steering him to a seat nearer the exit door. *I can't imagine the brazenness of these city women,* she was fuming inwardly.

They'd try to steal a woman's husband right out from under her very nose. Why, that's even worse than taking a watch! Clark seemed to remain unaware of the small hubbub as the two settled themselves on the bench together. Marty carefully avoided any eye contact with the woman across the station.

Someone finally called, "All aboard for points west," and Marty quickly stood, shook the wrinkles from her skirt, and straightened her hat. Clark gave her arm a reassuring squeeze and they moved with the crowd toward the waiting train.

Having never been on a train before, Marty was both excited and apprehensive. She found the high steps awkward to maneuver with her long skirt and was glad for Clark's helping hand as she climbed up.

Inside the train car, the rows and rows of seats were not as elegant as Marty had imagined they would be. The plush fabric was faded and even a little frayed in spots. Marty figured out that the fancier newer train cars would run between the large eastern cities.

They were jostled a bit as they sought a seat. Everyone seemed to be in a hurry to find a place, as though they were afraid the train might leave without them. Clark and

Marty found a seat quickly enough. They settled themselves and tucked their carry-along luggage under the seat. Marty sighed deeply. They had made it. Now if she only could get a glimpse of the sun to make sure this train was pointed in the right direction.

Gradually the commotion around them began to subside as other passengers settled in, as well. Marty noticed that not very many women had boarded the train. The men around them appeared to be of every type and station in life — from business-men to cattlemen, from miners to farmers like themselves, drifters and maybe even youngsters running away from home.

Marty shuddered as the scarlet plumes moved past them down the aisle and the woman from the station, with skirts and eyelashes fluttering, took a seat. She had selected a spot far from the other womenfolk in the car, among the men who had already pulled out a deck of cards and made them-selves a makeshift table. Great drifts of cigar and cigarette smoke already blurred the air around them. Marty hoped there would be no smokers in her area, but it was in vain. Not being used to smoke at all, Marty found it particularly trying. Were they to endure this all the way to Missie's? Already she felt about ready to choke, and they hadn't even left the station yet.

The train gave a long low sound like an anguished groan, and the squeaking wheels began to revolve slowly. They were on the way at last. To Marty's vexation, she still couldn't tell if they were headed in the right direction.

Gradually the train began to pick up momentum. The rough-looking buildings on the back streets of the town flashed past them now. Marty watched carriages and horsemen pulled up on side streets waiting for the train to pass by. Children called and waved, and dogs barked. The train's whistle blew in response, but it steadily moved on.

They left the town behind and moved out into the open countryside. Marty could not draw her gaze away from the window. Trees swished by them, cattle lifted tails and ran off bawling, horses snorted and swung away, blowing angrily, tails and manes flying. Still the train pounded on, wheels clickity-clacking and smokestack spewing forth great billows streaming by their window.

It's a wonder, that's what it is, thought Marty. *Why, I bet we're going about as fast as a horse can gallop, and nobody needs to lift a finger for the doing of it.* Though she probably would have gotten a vigorous argument if she had expressed such thoughts to the train engineer or coal stoker.

Marty finally took her eyes from the passing countryside long enough to look at Clark, interested in his reaction to this captivating new experience. To her amazement, she found that Clark had settled himself comfortably and, with head leaning back against the makeshift package of their food bundle, he slept soundly as though sleep was the full purpose of a train ride.

"Well, I never," muttered Marty under her breath and then smiled. She should be sleeping, too. The recent days had been most difficult and busy, and the sleep she had gotten in the last few nights was limited indeed. Clark was wise. He, too, was tired. He needed the rest. She'd try, as well. But, in spite of her resolve, she could not as yet get her mind or body to relax. She'd just watch the scenery for a while. Maybe she could sleep later.

Marty must have slept, for she aroused at the sound of a crying baby. It took her a few moments to get her bearings, and then excitement again filled her as she recalled that they were on the way to Missie.

The baby continued to cry. Marty opened her eyes and turned toward Clark. But when she looked, he was not there. For a moment, she was unnerved. Where could one disappear to on a moving train? Remembering the "lost-watch" scare of the morning, she told herself that Clark would not be far away and not to get in a dither.

The coach was even more blue with smoke than it had been when she had dropped off to sleep. It was hot and stuffy, too, and Marty longed for some fresh air. She gazed about her at the crowded coach. The poker game was still going on at the far end of the car. The woman had removed her brilliant hat, and she no longer sat alone. A distinguished gentleman in a fancy suit and frilly shirt was sitting with her. They laughed as they talked.

The crying baby was in the seat across the aisle. The poor mother already looked tired out. She had two other little ones with her, as well. The man who accompanied her growled to her to "hush the brat 'fore we git throwed off the train," and the woman tried even more intently to quiet the infant. But the baby was not to be placated. The man got up and, angrily muttering to himself, left. This started another one of the children crying, and the young mother really had her hands full. Marty started to leave her seat and go to the woman's aid, but a matronly looking woman arrived on the scene first.

"Can I help you some?" she asked the mother, and, without waiting for a reply, she took the crying baby. "You care for your son, and I'll try to get the baby to sleep."

Marty's heart went out to the young mother, and she said a quick prayer of thanks for the kind motherly soul who was helping. She laid the baby in her lap and loosened the blanket. The baby soon was sleeping, and Marty wondered if perhaps the young mother had bundled the little one too tightly and the poor infant was nearly smothering in the discomfort of the sun-heated coach.

Marty laid aside her own hat and tried to fan her flushed face. *What I wouldn't give to be able to go for a walk,* she thought. *Sure would feel good to have a little wind on one's face.*

Clark returned, and Marty was relieved in spite of her little inner lecture earlier.

"Feelin' a little better?" Clark asked.

"I did sleep some, an' it sure didn't do me no harm. Would be nice to cool off a mite. This here coach is so stuffy an' so filled with smoke, I feel like I'm travelin' in a saloon 'stead of a —"

"Now, what you be knowin' 'bout a saloon?"

"I don't, it's jest —"

But Clark was laughing at her.

"Where ya been?" asked Marty to change the conversation.

"Jest stretchin' my legs some. Ain't much of a place to walk, thet's fer sure. Jest back an' forth, back an' forth. S'pose it helped a little."

"What I wouldn't give fer a walk 'bout now," said Marty.

"Ya want fer me to ask 'em to stop the train an' let ya off fer a spell?"

"Clark . . ." But she didn't finish, and Clark stopped his teasing.

"What time is it, anyway?" asked Marty finally.

Clark pulled out his pocket watch. "Well, it's almost noon. Quarter of twelve, in fact."

Marty sighed heavily. "Thought it would be at least late afternoon," she said. "Seems like we been travelin' fer half of forever already."

Clark smiled.

"How many days did ya say we'd be on the train?"

"Reckon they didn't say fer sure. They was rather offhand about arrivin' time. Said thet the trip usually took 'bout a week — dependin' on the weather, the track, an' such."

"A week! I'm thinkin' we'll have us enough of this train by the time *thet* week is over."

68

"Well, now, I didn't say *this* train, exactly. We'll be leavin' this train in three days' time. We transfer to another one. This one's usually on time to where it's goin'. It's the one further on thet's some changeable."

"I didn't know thet we would be gettin' on another train. What'll it be like?"

"I'm not rightly sure. Only thing I know, it seems a bit unpredictable. But it won't be so bad. By the time we board her, we'll already be in the West an' almost there."

Marty suddenly felt hungry. "Anythin' still fittin' to eat in thet there pillow of yours?"

Clark passed her the lunch. It hadn't suffered much. Ellie had packed it well.

Marty lifted out a box that held sandwiches. "Sure would be glad fer a nice hot cup of tea or coffee," she commented.

"I think thet I jest might be able to find us some," said Clark and left his seat, walked down the aisle and out the swinging door. He was soon back with two steaming mugs of hot coffee. It was too strong for Marty's liking, but it was coffee and it did wash the smoke taste from her throat.

They finished their lunch with a couple of tarts, and Marty carefully repacked the uneaten food.

"Ya know, ya could stretch yer legs a bit iffen ya like to," offered Clark. "Seed other

69

women movin' 'bout some. An' the little room's down thet way," he motioned.

Marty smiled her thanks and stood up. She couldn't believe how rumpled her dress looked in just one morning. She tried to smooth the wrinkles out but they stubbornly remained, so she shrugged in resignation and moved out into the aisle.

Marty had been vaguely aware of the rock and sway of the train as she sat in her seat, but she had had no idea how decided it was until she took a step forward. The train suddenly seemed to lurch, throwing her off balance. She quickly put out a foot to rebalance herself when the train rolled the other way, leaving her startlingly off-balance again. Each place she went to put her foot was either too high or too low. At last she gave up trying to make it on her own and firmly grasped the seats as she moved forward. It seemed to be an awfully long walk to the "little room," and by the time Marty had made it back to Clark, she'd had enough of train-aisle walking for the time.

The train hooted and chugged, whined and rocked its way westward. Marty viewed more than one sunrise and sunset, happily content that the train was truly headed in the right direction.

They stopped at small towns to let off or

take on passengers. Sometimes the train seemed to sit for a ridiculously long time while train cars were shuffled and shouting men hauled off or on some sort of cargo. At these times Clark and Marty would leave the train and walk, strolling around just to get the kinks out of their muscles. On occasion they visited a store to restock their little food supply. Often it was no cooler out on the station platform than it had been in the stuffy coach, but at least it was a bit of relief from the cramped position. Marty began to wonder if it really would have been much more difficult to cover the miles in a jolting covered wagon.

The landscape around them changed with each passing day. Trees were fewer in number, often forlornly clumped together by a meandering stream. The towns, sometimes no more than a few scattered houses, were now even farther apart than before. On the third day, they rolled into a town that Clark announced was the place where they would transfer to the other train. Marty was not reluctant to make the change. She had no ties to this present train, and she had found very little in common with their fellow travelers. Those few whom she had become acquainted with all seemed to have gotten off at earlier stops except for the one middle-aged lady in dove-gray gown and hat who had helped with the baby. Mrs. Swanson was heading west to live with her son, her husband having died recently. Marty thought it was awfully spunky of the woman to make such a life-changing move all alone.

Clark had visited with several of the men on the train, attempting to learn all he could about the West before arriving at his son-in-law's ranch. He did not wish to appear to the ranch hands as another "ignorant fella from the East," he told Marty.

When they arrived at their point of transfer and the train dismissed its passengers, Clark and Marty found their way across the rough platform. People milled about and called to one another, but as there was no one in this town they knew, they kept their attention on the task of finding their luggage and getting it stored in readiness for the next train in the morning. Then they made their way from the station into town to find suitable lodging.

The baggage attendant had informed them that a hotel was just down the street within easy walking distance. When Clark requested a room from the man at the reception desk, he was told that a room was available and named the price. Marty was shocked when she heard the amount. But Clark did not argue with him and counted out the bills from the small roll he carried in his pocket.

They climbed worn carpeted stairs and found their room number. Marty looked about her in shock at the sight that confronted them on opening the battered door. The room was almost bare, except for a good bit of dirt and dust, and the bed linens appeared to have been used by at least one other occupant — maybe more. Marty had little objection to sparse furnishings, but actual grime was another matter.

Marty could see Clark eying the muddy boot prints on the floor and the soiled pillows strewn on the bed. But he made no remark on the sad state of the room.

"I think I'll take me a little walk an' sorta check out the town. Ya wanta come along or jest rest a bit?" asked Clark.

A walk did sound appealing, yet from what Marty had so far seen of the town, she was not so sure she wanted to investigate it.

"I think I'll jest rest here fer a bit. I'll see the town when we go out to git our supper," she answered.

Clark took his hat and left.

Marty didn't know what to do with herself after Clark had gone. She wished she had a broom, a pail of hot, soapy water, and a stiff scrub brush. The place looked as though it could use a good cleaning.

She crossed to the bed with the thought of lying down, but then eyed the soiled linen and changed her mind. She walked to the window, intending to pass some time by watching the action down on the street. The window looked out on nothing but the desolate countryside. She lifted her case from the only chair in the room, an over-stuffed piece that certainly had seen better days, and tried to settle herself in it. It had a broken spring that made it impossible to sit comfortably. Marty decided her only choice was to pace the floor. Well, she could certainly do with the exercise after being confined to the swaying train for three days. She walked. Round and round she walked, wishing she had gone with Clark.

About the time she thought she would surely go crazy, Clark returned, carrying clean bed linens over his arm.

"The maid has arrived," he joked.

"Where'd ya git those?" Marty asked admiringly. "Ya been foragin' through hotel closets?" she teased.

"Not exactly. They weren't all thet easy to come by. I went out fer a walk, like I said. There's only one other hotel, of a sort, in

74

this here town. It boasted 'bout bein' 'full up.' Couldn't find a decent roomin' house anywhere. So when I got back here, I jest asked the fella at the desk for some clean linens. I said it 'peared like the maid had somehow missed our room when she was makin' her rounds. He wasn't too happy to 'commodate me, but I jest stood right there, smilin' an' waitin'. He finally found me some."

Marty was happy to strip the bed and put on the clean sheets and cases.

"Not too much fer eatin' places, either," Clark continued as she worked. "Did see a small place down the street. Looks a little more like a saloon than a café, but it mightn't be too bad iffen we git there early an' leave as soon as we're done."

"We can go most anytime. I'll jest fix my hair some an' grab me a hat."

They left the hotel and walked out into the brisk wind. Marty held her hat with one hand and her skirt with the other.

"Fella I met says it blows like this most of the time here," remarked Clark as they leaned into the wind. Marty wondered what in the world the women did if they ever needed one of their hands free to carry something.

When they reached the unpretentious

building where they were to get their evening meal, Clark held the door against the wind. They seated themselves at a small table, and Clark nodded for the waiter. They soon learned that the "house speciality" was stew and biscuits; or roast beef, gravy, and biscuits; or beans, bacon, and biscuits. They ordered the roast beef and settled in to wait for their meal.

Marty glanced around the room. The lighting, a lone flickering lamp on each table, was dim. The few windows seemed to be covered with some kind of dark paint. A blue haze from the smoking of the occupants further hindered visibility. Most of those who lounged around were not eating but drinking. Marty did spot three men in the far corner who were having a meal. The others just seemed to be talking or playing cards. Occasionally a loud laugh would break the otherwise comparative silence in the place. At least for now, Marty was the only woman in the place.

Marty hoped their order would come quickly so they might leave soon. If this was Missie's West, Marty wasn't sure she would be at home in it. She felt uneasy in her present surroundings. Having never traveled beyond her own small community since leaving her girlhood home, Marty was very unfamiliar with the present environment. She had seen and heard things on this trip that were entirely new to her. She was sure she was not in favor of a lot of what she saw — the brashness, the intemperate drinking, the gambling, the casual attitude toward life and morality.

Their meal arrived. The waiter asked gruffly, "Watcha drinkin'?" as he set the plates down, frowning when Marty asked for tea. She hastily changed her order to coffee before he had time to respond. He didn't fuss about the coffee, but when he set it before her it was so old and strong she wasn't sure if she'd be able to drink it.

The meat was a little tough and the gravy was greasy and lumpy, but Marty sopped her biscuits in it and ate like the men in the corner. She was unable to finish it all and was relieved when she felt she had eaten enough that she could leave the rest. Clark had a second cup of coffee, and then they were free to go.

Forgetting it was still daylight, Marty was unprepared for the bright sunshine when they stepped out the door. She took advantage of the fact to study the buildings of the town and look in the store windows. The things on display did not really seem all that different from what Mr. Emory carried at the general store back home. The fact both surprised and relieved her. Perhaps Missie was able to shop for needed items after all.

It was too early to retire, so Clark suggested a short walk. Marty didn't like the wind but, remembering her confining attempt to walk in the dismal little room, she agreed. They walked on past the remainder of the buildings on the street — the bank, the sheriff's office, the telegraph office, another store, on past the stagecoach office to the feedstore, the livery, and the blacksmith. Clark slowed his steps to better watch the action at the smithy's. Two burly men were shouting and shoving as they prodded a big roan-colored ox into the ox sling for shoeing. The ox had decided on his own that he didn't need new shoes. Marty heard some words she didn't think were intended for a lady's ears, so she hastened her steps. Clark lengthened his stride to catch up to her.

Having eventually left the board sidewalks behind, the roadway was dusty and rough, but it felt good to walk full stride. Marty let go of her skirt, allowing the hem to swish the ground as she walked. The wind wasn't as strong now, or maybe she was just getting used to it. There didn't seem to be anyone else around, so she took off her hat, carrying it carefully in her hand, and let the wind tease at her hair. It felt good, and she wished for a moment she could reach up and pull the hairpins from it, as well, and shake it loose to blow free.

They left the street and turned onto a well-worn path. It led them into a grove of small trees; and, after walking for about fifteen minutes, they were surprised to discover a tiny stream that flowed rather sluggishly along. It wasn't like Marty's spring-fed creek back home, but it was water, and its discovery brought rest and joy to Marty's heart. She stooped to pick a few of the small flowers that grew along its banks.

Clark seemed to enjoy it, too. He stood and breathed deeply. "I wonder jest where it comes from," he murmured, "an' where it goes. This little bit thet we see here before us don't tell us much 'bout it a'tall. It could have started high up in the mountains as a ragin' glacier-fed river and been givin' of itself all across the miles until all thet is left is what we see here. Or it could go 'most from ocean to ocean by joinin' up with cousin waters thet eventually make it a mighty river. Someday it could carry barges or sailin' ships. Rather interestin' to ponder on, ain't it?"

Marty nodded and looked at the small stream with a new respect.

They lingered awhile, and then walked much more slowly back into town. On the way they watched the western sun sink below the far horizon with a wonderful display of vibrant colors.

"Well," sighed Marty, "I sure do favor me Missie's sunsets."

The hotel room looked just as bleak and bare when they again reached it, but Marty felt much better about having a clean bed. And she was sure enough ready for it now. After two nights on a swaying train, it would be good to have a solid place to lie down. They prepared for bed, prayed together, and crawled between the sheets. Clark put out the light, and before many minutes had passed, Marty knew he was sleeping soundly. She lay for a while thinking of the family at home and feeling just a bit lonely. Then she thought of Missie and her family, and the lonely feeling slipped away as she, too, drifted off to sleep.

Sometime during the night Marty awoke. Something was wrong. Something had wakened her. Was it a noise of some sort? No, she didn't remember hearing anything out of the ordinary. Clark stirred. He seemed restless, too. Marty turned over and tried to go back to sleep. It didn't work. She turned again.

"You havin' problems, too?" asked Clark softly.

"Can't sleep," Marty complained. "Don't rightly know why, I jest —"

"Me too."

They tossed and turned as the minutes ticked slowly by.

"What time is it?" asked Marty. "Anywhere near mornin'? Might as well git up an' be done with it iffen it is."

Clark reached for his watch. He couldn't read the hands in the darkness.

"Mind iffen I light the lamp to git a look?"

"Go ahead. Lamplight ain't gonna make me any wider awake than I am already."

Clark struck a match and lit the lamp. As the soft glow spread over the bed, Marty gasped. Clark, who had moved the pocket watch into the light to get a look at the time, jerked his head up.

"Bedbugs!" exclaimed Marty.

Both of them were instantly on their feet, and many small insects darted for cover.

"Bedbugs! No wonder we couldn't sleep! Oh, Clark! We'll be scratchin' our way all across these prairies."

"Funny," said Clark, "I never felt 'em bitin' me."

"Thet's the way with bedbugs. Sometimes ya don't even feel 'em until the bite starts to swell up an' itch. You'll feel 'em fer sure tomorrow, I'm thinkin'."

Marty ran to check their cases and thankfully noted that they were tightly closed. Only their bodies and the clothing around the room to worry about.

"Clark, when we leave this here place, we gotta be awful sure we don't take none of them with us."

"An' how we gonna do thet?"

"I'm not rightly sure. One thing I do know — thet light stays on fer the rest of the night, an' I'm not crawlin' back into thet bed."

They washed carefully, then inspected each item of their clothing before they put it on. Marty brushed and brushed and brushed her hair in the hopes that if there were any of the little creatures in her hair, she would brush them out. None appeared. She didn't quite know whether that was a good sign or a bad one.

After checking and rechecking, they packed their belongings carefully and closed the cases tightly. Marty put the cases as close to the lamp as she could and stood vigil. It was still only four o'clock . . . hardly the hour of the morning to take to the street.

They managed to wait until the first rays of the dawn were showing on the eastern horizon, and then they left the hotel. The room had been paid for in advance, so Clark just tossed the key on the desk; the sleeping clerk stirred slightly, murmured something inaudible, and settled back to snoring. They walked through the unpainted doors and out into the street.

"Where are we gonna go?" questioned Marty. "Nothin' will be open yet."

"Well, there's a bench over there in front of the sheriff's office. How 'bout sittin' in the sun fer a spell?"

Marty nodded. It was a bit cool in the morning air; she could do with a little sun. She hoped that the warmth of the rays would reach them quickly.

It was a while before others were also stirring about the streets of the town. The livery hand arrived first and went about the duties of feeding the horses and a pair of mules. Roughly dressed men eventually swaggered out of the hotel, a few at a time; then the blacksmith began pounding on some metal in his shop. Shop owners began to open doors and rearrange window signs. The sheriff checked his office and then headed for the hotel and a cup of morning coffee. There was more movement toward the hotel, and soon Marty and Clark could smell cooking bacon and brewing coffee. Marty had not realized she was hungry until that moment.

Clark turned toward her. "Rather fun to watch a town wake up. I've never done thet before," he commented, and Marty nodded her head in agreement.

"It's not really so different from home as far as looks go — yet it *feels* strange," she answered. "Still, I haven't seen anything —" Her words were interrupted.

Four cowboys rode into view, their horses dusty and tired. They led four other horses behind them with some kind of bundles tied on their backs. The horses were spotted and wore no saddles, although two of them had colorful blankets tossed across their backs. The men rode past silently, their leather-encased feet swinging freely and their hair hanging past their shoulders in long black braids. Upon observing the braids, Marty snatched a second look. Why, those weren't cowboys. They were Indians! Now *that* was different. The riders looked neither to the left nor the right as they rode down the street and pulled their mounts to a stop before the general store. They swung down from their horses and began to untie the bundles from the backs of the pack animals.

"Looks like they've got 'em a pretty good catch of furs," observed Clark.

"Furs," said Marty. "I never thought of furs. What kind, ya supposin'?"

"I've no idea. Coyotes, badgers, maybe. Not close enough to the mountains fer bears or wildcats, I'm thinkin'. But then I'm not much fer knowin' jest what they do have hereabouts."

Marty turned only after they had all disappeared.

"Well," said Clark, "ya ready fer some breakfast?" He stood up and stretched his tall frame.

Marty stood, too, and picked up her lunch bundle and hatbox. Without thinking, she reached to scratch an itching spot on her rib cage, then checked herself; a lady did not go about scratching in public. At the same time, she realized that Clark was scratching his neck. Marty looked at the spot. "Oh my," she whispered.

Clark looked at her.

"Ya sure enough got yer share," stated Marty. "They're beginnin' to show up all along yer collar."

"Bedbugs?"

"Bedbugs. Well, not the bugs exactly — but where they been."

"Guess they liked me better'n they did

you, huh?"

" 'Fraid not," said Marty. "I got me four or five places thet I'd jest *love* to be scratchin'."

Clark laughed. "Well, maybe a cup of coffee an' a slice of ham will take our mind off 'em." He picked up the cases and motioned Marty toward the hotel's dining room they had passed up the night before in favor of the saloon place.

"Fella told me thet this ain't the fanciest place around; but it's the only one thet's open this time of the day, so I guess we'll give it a try. Surely nobody can make too much of a mess outta just boilin' coffee."

Maybe Marty was just hungry, or maybe the food actually wasn't so bad; at any rate, she ate heartily.

Six
Arrival

The next three days on the train, a very slow-moving one, were even more difficult for Marty. For one thing, she was in a fever to reach Missie, and the many delays and the hesitant forward crawl irritated her. She also was tired from several nights without a good rest, and the train they rode was even more primitive and worn than the first. The wooden seats and cramped quarters made it difficult to sit comfortably, and the narrow aisles allowed little room for stretching or walking.

There were only two other women on the crowded train, and neither seemed inclined to make new friendships. The men, rough and rugged, appeared mostly to be gold seekers or opportunists. The constant smoking of cigars and cigarettes made Marty feel like choking. The temperature continued to climb, and the heat and stuffiness of the car almost overcame her. Discovering the bedbug bites from their previous hotel room did not help her frame of mind. Occasionally there was something of interest out the train window, like the small herd of buffalo that wandered aimlessly along beside the track. But usually there was nothing at all to see but barren hills and windswept prairie. Now and then herds of cattle or a squatter's makeshift buildings came into view. Marty counted only three *real* houses, each surrounded by many outbuildings. She guessed each of these to be someone's profitable ranch.

The small towns along the route, though few and far between, looked very busy. Marty wondered where the people came from. As much as she normally enjoyed watching people, she did not care for that activity now. She just wanted to get to the LaHaye ranch and Missie, and each time the train stopped and frittered away precious time, Marty chafed inside. What could they possibly be doing to take so long in such an insignificant place, anyway? Marty fussed, minding the heat, the cramped quarters, the smoke, the delay, and the itching bites.

But all her fretting did not get them one mile closer to Missie, she gradually came to realize. At length Marty willed herself to take a lesson from Clark and learn some patience. She settled herself in her corner and determined not to stew. She even decided to study the countryside and see what she could learn about it.

Early on the third morning, Clark returned from chatting with a fellow in a seat farther up the coach and informed Marty with a grin that the man had said Missie's small town was the next stop, and unless something unforeseen happened, they should be in by noon. Marty was wild with joy. Now it was even harder to sit still and not chafe about the slowpoke engine that took them forward at such a snail's pace.

The man was right. Just before the noon hour the train began to slow, and they all stirred themselves and started to gather their belongings.

Marty cast one final look around at her fellow passengers. She noticed a youth hoist up his small bundle and move toward the door. He looked tired and hungry, and there was a bit of uncertainty and loneliness in his eyes.

Why, he don't look any older than my Luke, Marty thought compassionately. *Supposin' he's come on out here all by himself an' don't know where he's goin' or what he'll find when he gits there?*

Marty was about to ask Clark if there was something they could do for the youth when the train stopped and the boy disappeared in the crowd.

They climbed down the steps from the train, looked around quickly, and moved toward the dusty new sidewalk. The boards had not fully weathered yet, and they obviously were newer than the town. Marty noticed the buildings were recently built, but many of them looked as though they had been constructed in a big hurry with the cheapest material available. Little attention was given to fanciness or even getting things straight.

Marty's eyes turned to the scores and scores of bawling cattle milling around in the corrals to the right of the tracks, kicking up dust and drowning out all other noises. Yes, this was a cattle town, to be sure.

But Marty really was not interested in buildings or cattle — only people. She was busy scanning the crowd for a glimpse of Missie.

Dust-covered cowboys — and equally dust-covered horses — moved back and forth on the main street, wide hats almost hiding their features. A number of women walked by, none of them in hats but wearing cheap and practical bonnets or nothing on their heads at all.

Marty was trying to stay close to Clark through the crushing passengers from the incoming train, all the while straining her eyes for the first sight of Missie, when a deep voice drawled beside them, " 'Scuse me, sir, but are you folks the Davises?"

Marty looked up at the cowboy who stood beside them, hat in hand.

"Shore are," replied Clark.

"Right glad to meet ya, sir — ma'am. I'm Scottie, foreman for the LaHayes, an' I been sent to meet this here train." Marty felt her heart sink with disappointment. Missie was not here.

Clark set down a case so he could extend a hand. "Glad to meet ya, Mr. Scott."

"I'd be happy to take ya on over to the hotel, ma'am, and let ya freshen up some. It's gonna be a bit of a ride to the ranch. Then we'll collect yer things an' be off."

"I'd like thet," replied Marty as cheerfully as she could, and they followed Scottie down the street.

"Mrs. LaHaye is 'most bustin' with eagerness. She could hardly stand it thet she ain't here to meet ya herself. Never know when this here train is finally gonna pull in. This one was scheduled to be in here yesterday. 'Course, one day late ain't so bad. Sometimes it's been as much as five. A little hard fer her to stand around waitin' with two little ones in tow — ya know what I mean?"

But Scottie didn't wait for an answer.

"Boss, he came into town to check yesterday — brought the whole family, jest in case the train happened to be on time. Well, she warn't. He sent me on in today. He was gonna give it another try tomorra. Missus will be right glad thet it won't be necessary."

Marty was glad, too. *Mercy me,* she thought, *I'da never stood it if we'd been five days late — and neither would poor Missie!*

They entered the small hotel, and Scottie spoke to the man at the desk. Marty was shown to a room. It was not fancy, but it was clean. Marty was glad for a fresh supply of water for a good wash. The men left again to go pick up their baggage from the train station. Marty prayed that everything had arrived safely and intact.

She couldn't help but feel some disappointment at the further delay. She had thought when she arrived in this little town that her long wait to see Missie would be over. But of course Scottie was right. It would have been very foolish for Missie to make the long trip every day, not having any idea when the train might actually arrive.

The room seemed cool in spite of the warm weather, and after Marty's wash she lay down on the bed, promising herself that she'd just rest for a few minutes while she waited for Clark and Mr. Scottie to come.

The next thing she knew Clark was bending over her. He said Scottie was ready to take them for a little something to eat before they headed for the ranch.

Despite Marty's hunger, she begrudged even the time spent on the meal. They hurried with their dinner because Scottie, too, was anxious to get back to the ranch.

Marty sat in the wagon on a seat that had been especially fashioned for her by Willie and made as comfortable as possible. Clark sat up on the driver's bench with Scottie. Scottie was not a great talker, but he was generous in answering any questions. Marty paid no attention to the conversation. Nor did she particularly watch the passing scenery. Her mind was totally on Missie, wondering how much reserve the passing years might have put between mother and daughter. Would they still be able to share feelings and thoughts, or would the time and the experiences have closed some doors for them? Marty felt a little fear grip at her heart. And what about Missie's children, her grandchildren? Would they see her as only a stranger they did not particularly welcome to their world? The questions and doubts persisted until her mind was whirling with anxieties as they rumbled along. Clark turned back to check on her now and then, and she managed to give him a shaky smile. She hoped he didn't notice her agitation.

And then they came over a hill, and Scottie pulled up the team. "There's the boss's spread, right down there," he said, pride coloring his voice. It was evident he felt a measure of ownership in the ranch, just by his association. Marty's heart skipped. Right down there! Right before her very eyes was their Missie's home. Marty saw a large, sprawling, gray stone home. Soft smoke curled up from the chimney. Off to one side, she could see a garden and a very small stream flowing away from a rocky embankment. She let her eyes seek out the pen with the chickens, the seeming miles of corrals, the bunkhouse and cook shack, and, yes, there on the other side was a straw-colored mound. *That must be Missie's soddy.* Marty's eyes filled with tears, and she had an impulse to jump from the wagon and run down the hill. Remarkably, she held herself in check. Scottie clucked to the team, and they moved forward.

Whether it was Scottie's driving or Marty's wishful thinking or the eagerness of the team to return to their stalls, Marty never knew for sure. But the remainder of the trip down the long winding hill went more quickly.

At the bottom of the hill, Scottie "whoaed" the horses and handed the reins to Clark. "I'll jest be gettin' on back to my duties," he said. "You'll be wantin' to make yer greetin's in private," he added as he stepped down from the wagon.

"And many thanks to ya fer yer welcome an' fer drivin' us this long way," Clark said warmly. Scottie tipped his hat to them and moved off toward the barn. Marty climbed up beside Clark for a better view of the house as the horses moved forward. A flash of red calico in a window, and then . . . there was Missie, her arms opened wide and her face shining with tears, running toward them calling their names. Marty ran to embrace her beloved daughter. They held each other close, crying and laughing and repeating over and over tender, senseless endearments.

At last, at last, sang Marty's heart. *At last I have my "if only."*

■ ■ ■ ■

The hours that followed were wild with excited chatter and activity. The two grandsons had immediately captivated their newfound grandparents. Marty was so thankful that the boys moved forward without hesitation and even allowed hugging. Nathan beamed his pleasure. He was all ready to take charge of the entertainment of these two special people in his mother's life. "Mama said I could show ya my room," and "Mama said you'd go ridin' with me, Grandpa," and "Mama said you'd like to see my own pony," and "Mama said you'd read to me sometimes." Missie laughed, and Marty realized she had been carefully preparing her children for the adventure of meeting their grandparents.

Josiah was too young to be as active in the conversation, but he pulled at coattails and hands and insisted on "Up!" Marty was thrilled with how quickly the two little boys felt at ease with their grandparents. When Josiah did manage to steal a scene from Nathan, he was full of chatter of "See this" and "Do you like my . . . ?" and "Lookit, G'amma." For Clark and Marty, their hearts were captured at sight by the two small boys.

The whole house was filled with happy sounds as Missie proudly showed them from room to room. Marty exclaimed over the comfort, the coolness, and the attractiveness of the big stone house. They had entered through wide double doors into a large cool hall. The floor was of polished stone, and the inside walls were textured white stucco. Missie had used paintings with Spanish-Mexican influence to decorate the walls and had placed an old Spanish bench of white wrought iron against one wall. The bench had cushions of a flower-print material, and Missie had picked up the shade of green in them to highlight little finishing touches in the room, a pleasing and cool effect. The living room was large and airy with a mammoth stone fireplace and deep red and gold fabrics on the furnishings. The draperies, of matching material, were tied back with gold cords. It looked Spanish *and* — thought Marty — *very rich and inviting.* The floor was dark-stained wood, and the walls were, like the entry, textured stucco. Scattered across the polished wooden floors were deep-colored rugs — not the home-made variety but store bought. The pictures and lamps were Spanish — and elegant, with blacks, reds, and golds predominant. Marty viewed her surroundings in awe.

Never had she seen such a grand living room, she told Missie.

On they moved to the dining area. "And," said Missie, with a wave of her hand and a laugh, "that's as far as we've been able to go with our grandness. From here on, it's common living. But it'll come together, little by little, with each cattle shipment."

Missie gestured toward a long homemade trestle table that easily seated eight. "Willie has promised me some dining room chairs and a *real* table this fall." Though the chairs looked comfortable enough, they were not matched or of particular quality. The white-stuccoed walls were quite bare, and inexpensive curtains hung at the windows. A simple cabinet against the far wall held the good dishes that Marty had insisted Missie take west. Somehow the simple, homey room put Marty's heart at ease. The differences now between them might not be so great after all.

"Oh, Missie, I'm so proud of you and so happy for you!" she exclaimed with a quick hug. Clark's approving grin echoed that sentiment.

The bedrooms were all big and roomy, but again, the furnishings here were simple and the curtains and spreads and the rugs on the floor were all homemade. Marty recognized many things she had helped to sew.

Missie led them to the other wing, the kitchen area of the house. Marty was surprised when Missie stopped at the door and gave a brief rap, then walked in. A wiry little Chinese man was busily engaged in preparations for the evening meal. Marty had not known that Missie had a cook.

"Wong," said Missie, "this is my pa, my mama."

The Chinese man favored them with a big grin and bobbed his head up and down as he acknowledged the introductions.

"How'do, how'do," he said over and over. "Wong pleased with pleasure. How'do, how'do."

Clark and Marty both answered with smiles and greetings.

"Wong is trying hard to learn our difficult English," Missie explained while Wong beamed at them. "He has done very well in a short time. He does not need to learn how to cook. He knew all about cooking when he came. Every rancher hereabouts envies us and hopes for an invitation often to eat his delicious food."

Wong bobbed his head again and led them around the large kitchen. Marty had never seen so much working room. The stove was big, too, and Wong proudly lifted the covers from several steaming kettles, all sending forth delicious fragrances.

Missie led her parents down a hall and toward a back door.

"I had me no idea thet ya had a cook. My, my," remarked Marty.

"Wong has not been with us for long," Missie answered. "At first, I thought Willie was being silly to suggest it, but I wonder now why I even tried to fight it. Wong is so much help. He helps with the laundry, too. It gives me more time for the children, and I still have plenty to keep me busy with this big house. I'm glad that we have him — and it gives him a job and a home, as well. Nathan and Josiah adore him. But it made Cookie terribly jealous at first," Missie continued. "He was so afraid that someone else would take his place with our boys. But the two rascals have managed to keep both of the men happy. Actually, the two cooks seem to really enjoy each other now. Most evenings they get together for a cup of coffee and a chat. In fact, Cookie is the one who volunteered to teach English to Wong."

Missie's long speech had brought them to the patio at the back of the house. The front, the bedroom wing on the one side, and the kitchen wing on the other surrounded this lovely area on three sides. The fourth side looked out toward the spring beyond Missie's flower beds. When Marty remarked on their beauty, Missie informed her that they were all flowers she had taken from the neighboring hills, except for the bed of roses. Scottie, a little red-faced with embarassment, had presented her with the roses when he had returned from purchasing some choice livestock farther south.

The sheltered veranda between the patio and the house was shaded and cool in the late afternoon. Marty imagined what a pleasant place this would be to spend an afternoon sewing or reading to the children. She was very impressed with the home Willie had built for Missie. Marty was pleased with their good taste, and she admired Missie's choice of color and texture in the living room. Also, it all said to Marty that times were good, that Missie and Willie were making upward strides after their primitive start in the soddy. The homier simple furnishings in the remainder of the house also spoke to Marty. These told her that Missie and Willie were willing to wait, to build gradually, to not demand everything at once, showing maturity and good judgment. Marty *was* proud of them — both of them.

After the tour through the house, Willie invited Clark out to see the barns and stock, and Missie took Marty to show her the garden, the spring, her chickens, and then the little soddy.

Nathan, who clung to Grandma's hand, didn't like to leave her to go with the men, but he was most anxious to show off his pony. Josiah, who had been riding on Grandpa's shoulder, hated to climb down but did not want to get too far away from his mother. Besides, he absolutely adored the chickens! After some complaints from both of the children, the three "men" headed for the barn, and the women and the younger son took the path to the garden.

Marty was pleased at the sight of Missie's garden. True, it wasn't as far along as her own had been on the farm back east, but the plants looked healthy and productive, and Marty could see that many good meals would be coming from the little patch.

The water from the spring was not as ambitious as the spring back home, but the effect it had on the surrounding area outweighed the difference. All around were brown hills and windswept prairies, but near the spring crowded green growing things and small shivery-leafed trees — truly an "oasis."

Missie briskly led the way to the chicken pen. Forty or fifty hens squawked and squabbled in the enclosure. They looked healthy enough, and Missie assured her mother that they were very good egg producers.

Josiah immediately began hollering at the chickens, attempting to throw handfuls of grass and dirt at them through the wire. Since the wind was blowing from the wrong direction, most of it blew right back into Josiah's face, so Missie put a stop to the activity. Josiah was quick to obey, blinking dust from his eyes.

As they moved on toward the unassuming soddy, Marty noticed that Missie referred to it with love and even joy, a fact that Marty found very difficult to understand. Missie pushed open the rough wooden door and they entered the dim little sod shack. When Marty's eyes had adjusted, she could make out the bed in the corner, the black iron stove right where it had been, the small table, and the two stools.

Marty gazed all around her, from the simple furnishings to the sod roof and the packed-dirt floor.

This is the "home" that waited for you after that long, hard trip? And you actually lived here, Marty thought incredulously. *You actually lived in this little shack — and with a new baby! How could you ever do it? How could you stand to live in such a way? My, I...*

But Missie was speaking: "Willie wanted to tear it down, to get it out of here, but I wouldn't hear tell. I've got a lot of memories in this little place. We've had to resod the roof a couple of times. Roofs don't last too long with the winter storms, the wind and rain. And once they start to leak, they aren't good for anything."

Marty did not express her feelings about the soddy. Instead she expressed her feeling for her girl. "I'm so proud of you, Missie — so proud. I hoped to bring ya up to be able to make a happy home fer the one thet ya learned to love. An' ya did. Ya looked beyond these here dirt walls into the true heart of the home. Home ain't fancy dishes an' such, Missie. Home is love and carin'. Remember when I insisted on those fancy dishes, Missie? I said thet you'd be so glad fer them someday. So I fussed 'bout ya takin' 'em, even though ya really had no room fer 'em an' could've taken somethin' more sensible in the little space you had in the wagon. Well, I was wrong, Missie." Marty's hand touched her daughter's cheek. "I was wrong, an' you were right. Home ain't dishes, frills, an' such, Missie. Home is love an' carin'. You showed me thet ya could truly make a home, an' ya could do it with jest yer own hands an' yer own heart. I'm proud of ya. So very proud."

Missie's answering smile was understanding as Marty wiped the tears from her eyes. She looked around once more before leaving the small soddy. This time it did not look as bleak nor the floor as earthy. In those few short minutes, something had happened that changed the appearance of the little room.

SEVEN
CATCHING UP

After insisting on a story from both Grandma and Grandpa, the children were finally tucked into bed for the night. Clark and Willie moved into his office, a small room off the kitchen, to discuss the business of farming and ranching. Missie and Marty settled comfortably in the living room with coffee cups.

"It was useless to try to 'catch up' before this," said Missie, "but I think things are quiet enough now for us to talk — really talk. I have so many questions. I just want to know about everyone — everyone. I hardly know where to start, but you might as well start talking, because I just can't bear to let you go to bed until I find out all about those at home."

Marty drew a deep breath. "I've been jest 'bout dyin' to tell ya all 'bout the family. My, ya'd be surprised iffen ya could see yer brothers an' sisters now!"

"Is big Clare still the tease?"

"Worse . . . worse, seems to me. He's always funnin', and I sometimes wonder if-fen he'll ever grow up. Yer pa says he will, once he marries an' settles down."

"And what is his Kate like? Clare wrote to me. Sounded in the letter as though she was nothing less than an angel sent from heaven. What's she really like?"

"Kate's a fine girl. We feel she's jest what Clare needs. She's quiet and steady, a little overly cautious at times, but they should balance each other real well. She's quite tall, with brown hair, large violet eyes . . . I think it was the violet eyes thet caught Clare's 'tention. Though she's not what ya'd call a beauty, she does have very pretty eyes."

"And you said they're going to marry this fall?"

"August twenty-seventh. Might have been a little sooner, but we wanted to be sure and have lots of time to get home again and git us ready fer the big event."

"Does Arnie have a girl?"

"He's been callin' on a little gal over in Donavan County. You remember Arnie — he's more the shy type. He takes things pretty slow like. Ellie says thet Hester will need to do the proposin' iffen it ever gits done!" Marty chuckled. "I think Arnie jest hasn't quite made up his mind yet. Wants to be good an' sure. She's a nice little girl, but her brothers are rather no-goods. Have a bad reputation in the area. Arnie ain't 'bout to let thet influence him, but he feels it's important when one marries to accept all the family members."

"Sometimes that just isn't possible," remarked Missie.

"Well, Arnie feels thet with Hester it has to be. She is very protective of her brothers. Would fight fer 'em if necessary. Arnie admires thet in her. But he wants to see the good in 'em that Hester sees. So far," Marty laughed softly, "I think he's been hard pressed to find some good, even though he's sure been lookin'."

"I hope he doesn't spend too many years *looking* and in the meantime let some girl with no such problems be snatched up by someone else."

Marty sighed. "Arnie deserves a good girl. He's so sensitive to the feelin's of others. He's got a lot of his father in him, thet boy."

"What about Ellie? Does she have a beau yet?"

"Not really. Not yet. Guess I was sorta hopin' ya wouldn't ask. I keep tryin' to pretend thet she ain't old enough yet — but I guess I know better, deep down. She's old enough. She's pretty enough, too. I guess she jest hasn't encouraged them much to this point. Ma Graham remarked 'bout her soon marryin' an' leavin' me. She's right. I've seen the boys tryin' to git her attention in a dozen ways. I always jest thought of it as schoolboy stuff. Not really. One of these days she'll notice 'em, too."

"Wish I could see her," Missie said, the yearning clear in her voice. "I suppose there would not be any chance she could come out and stay with us for a while?"

Marty felt a moment of panic. *Ellie come out here? The West is full of young men. Why, if she came to see her older sister, she might marry and never return home again!* Marty fought back her uncomfortable thoughts and responded in an even voice, "Maybe she could come on out on her honeymoon."

"But you said she didn't even have a beau —"

"She don't yet. But, my, thet can happen fast enough. I'm half scared she'll have her mind all made up 'bout some young fella by the time I git back home."

Missie laughed. "Now, I hardly think that's possible. Not for the short time you'll be away. Are you sure you can only stay for two weeks? Seems hardly worth coming all this way for such a short time."

"We couldn't possibly stay longer. Takes a week to come out an' a week to go home. By the time we git back, we'll have been gone a whole month. It's a busy time of the year, ya know. Pa left his boys completely on their own fer the summer hayin' an' all, an' Clare has to git his house ready. Luke is studyin' hard for his college exams an' —"

"Dear little Luke." Missie's voice was gentle. "How is he?"

A softness filled Marty's eyes. "He's not changed. Growed a little, I guess, but he's still got his same ways. Remember how he liked to cuddle up close in your lap when he was a young'un? Well, I git the feelin' sometimes he'd still like to do thet — iffen society wouldn't condemn it. He finds other ways to show love now. 'Member how you always used to pick me birthday strawberries? Well, yer pa broke up the pasture where the strawberries grew so well, so the last couple a' years the kids have jest forgot the strawberries. This year Luke decided thet I needed my birthday berries, so he went out real early an' went lookin' fer 'em. Had to really work hard, but he came back with a cupful. They was little and a mite on the green side, but I never tasted any better berries — ever."

"An' he's still doing well in school?"

"He's a good student, but he's through at the local school now. The teacher says she's given him everythin' she can give. He's read everythin' in sight an' still can't git enough."

"What will he do? He can't just quit."

"He plans to go on. Wants to go to the city fer college. I'm glad . . . an' scared . . . an' sad. All at the one time. I hate to see him go off alone like thet. Seems so young. He's only fifteen."

"Is he plannin' to be a teacher?"

Marty paused a moment before answering. "A doctor."

"A doctor?" Missie's tone was both surprised and admiring.

"He's had his heart set on it for a number of years now. He's talked to Doc Watkins 'bout it, too. Doc is pleased as a pappy. He doesn't have any children of his own, an' he's takin' great pleasure in nursin' Luke's ambitions."

"That would be nice to have a doctor in the family."

"Luke says he wants to help people. He's always wanted to help people, an' with so many towns not havin' a doctor —"

"What I wouldn't give to have a doctor here," Missie broke in, her tone wistful. "Young boy of our neighbor broke his arm last year. There was no one to set it properly.

He'll always have a twisted, almost useless arm, just because . . ." Missie's words trailed off. "I keep thinking, what if it had been Nathan?"

Marty looked at her daughter and understood. She knew a mother's heart and the panic when a doctor is nowhere around when one is sorely needed. She, too, breathed a prayer that somehow this frontier settlement might soon have a doctor, but she also added silently, *Not Lukey. Please, not Luke.*

Missie interrupted her thoughts and her unspoken prayers. "How are Nandry's and Clae's families?"

Marty was happy to report on the two Larson girls who had joined the Davis family when Missie was just a youngster. Marty spoke lovingly of the grandchildren who brought such joy and delightful commotion to family gatherings. "Nathan and Josiah would have sech fun with all their cousins," she noted.

"Tell me about the neighbors," Missie said. "Do we still have the same people living round about?"

"Pretty much. The Coffins moved on back to the area where they came from. Mrs. Coffin never really did take to our community. Some said she jest couldn't stand bein' away from her twin sister. After they lost their little girl — remember the sickly little one? — well, after they lost her, Mrs. Coffin insisted they go on back to their home. Some new people on their land now. Called the Kentworths. Not friendly folk at all. All the neighbors have tried to git acquainted an' have been told not to bother. People say thet he's a lawbreaker an' jest doesn't want folks snoopin' round. Thet's what he calls it when anyone comes visitin' — snoopin' round. She's 'most as bitter and disagreeable as he is, so fer the time we jest have to sit tight an' pray fer 'em and watch fer a chance to show our carin'. Must be awful to live with such inner bitterness."

Missie nodded her head thoughtfully in agreement.

Marty went on, "Most of the other neighbors are the same as before, I guess. The Grahams are as dear friends as ever. Sally Anne has three girls, 'most growed up now.

"Tommie's Fran jest had a baby boy. He's six years younger than Tom, Junior, the boy who had been the baby fer a good while. Tom is thrilled with the new little fella."

"And the Marshalls? How are they doing?"

"It's sad," Marty answered, "sad to see the Marshalls an' their son, but it's beautiful, too. There is so much love there. Rett is a very loving child. He's a young man really, but he is still a child. Wanda and Cam really love 'im. He is so good with animals thet it's 'most uncanny. Wild or tame — they all seem to understand and trust Rett."

"And Wanda's happy?"

"Happy? Yah, she's happy. She needs to rely on her God daily, though. She has her hard times, but I'm sure she wouldn't be tradin' her boy fer all the boys in town."

Missie shook her head as she thought of the grief Wanda had carried. "She has suffered so much," she said softly.

"Yah," acknowledged Marty, "she has suffered — suffered and growed. Sometimes it seems to take the one to bring the other."

"When one does suffer, it is good to see that it hasn't been wasted — that the sufferer allows God to make it a blessing rather than a bitterness," Missie observed.

Marty nodded and then went on. "Wanda and Ma Graham both sent their love. They sent some small gifts to ya, too. We have some packages from them in the trunk. Pa and I decided the things we brought with us would jest wait until tomorra. No sense rushin' into everythin' tonight."

"Now that you've mentioned gifts, I'm not sure I can wait till morning," Missie laughed. "Kind of like teasing a body —"

"They'll keep," Marty assured her, thinking Missie was still curious and excited about things just like old times at home. "We didn't want to come rushin' in here handin' out goodies right an' left. You might have understood, but Nathan and Josiah might be thinkin' thet's all grandparents are fer."

Missie laughed. "I'm thinking my sons have you both sorted out already. They seem to know right off that you're here just to spoil them."

"We'll have to be careful, but it sure'd be easy to spoil a bit, all right. Clae's girl, Esther Sue, and Nandry's four shore think thet we are there jest to humor them. 'Course they like attention from their uncles, as well. Arnie does most of the fussin'. Arnie really loves young'uns. The others all love the little ones, too, but it is Arnie who never seems to tire of 'em, though he pretends he does."

"And Joe still hasn't gone off to seminary? Has he changed his mind?"

"Oh no. He's as set on it as ever. I'm hopin' he'll be able to go next year."

"Oh, it's so good to catch up a bit! Makes me feel closer to them somehow. I've missed them all so much."

Marty's eyes filled with tears. "An' we've missed you. Missie, you'll never know how many —" She shook her head and stopped short. "No, I won't say it. I'm here now with you. I see ya have a lovely home, two beautiful boys, thet you're happy. I've told the Lord so many times thet if He'd jest give me this special treat, I'd thank Him with great thankfulness. Now I'm here an' I'm gonna keep my promise. I *am* thankful, Missie — so very thankful." Tears finally spilled down Marty's face, and Missie went to kneel before her and put her arms around her.

"Oh, Mama," she said, tears shining in her own eyes, "I've longed for you so often. I promised the Lord that I'd be content with seeing you, too. And here I've already been upset because you can't stay longer. I'm ashamed of myself. We'll just make every minute we have together count. We'll fill our time with so much happiness that we'll have barrels of memories to keep us when the time comes that we need to part again."

Marty smoothed Missie's hair. "Thet sounds like a grand idea," she said. "I've tucked away a few of these precious memories already."

Missie stood up. "Well," she said, "let's just get on with another one. Willie has

116

developed a real liking for popcorn before bed, so let's go pop some. He says there just isn't anything better than to have a close family chat over popcorn. It's warm, and homey, and filling." Missie laughed and led the way to the big kitchen. "I always feel like a little girl sneaking in where her mama doesn't want her when I do this. Wong is so fussy. But I always clean up very carefully." Mother and daughter laughed together.

The popcorn was soon ready, and Clark and Willie were called to join them in the living room. The visiting continued, as Willie and Missie asked all about the neighbors, the school, the church. Fighting emotion, Willie wanted to know how his pa, Zeke La-Haye, *really* was doing. The occasional letter somehow didn't seem to tell the whole story.

"I think a trip on out here would do him a world of good," Clark commented. "He needs to get a fresh outlook on things. Oh, he still loves his farm, but yer brother has 'most taken over now. Zeke loves his grandkids, too, but he still misses yer ma somethin' awful. He sent a little parcel along with us."

"All of this talk of parcels and presents from back home — and they plan to make us wait until morning!" Missie obviously could hold back her frustration no longer. "How can a body sleep tonight not knowing what's in the trunk?"

After some laughter and teasing, it was decided that the trunk and its contents would be brought in and distributed before retiring.

After the trunk was placed in the room and the straps removed, Missie dove in with a will, laying to one side those things intended for the children. She squealed and cried by turn, enjoying every item that had come with love from those "back home."

"We'll have Nandry's raspberry preserves for breakfast," she declared, holding up a sparkling jar.

The hour was late when they finally cleared up the clutter and said good-night with hugs all around.

Marty went to bed with an overflowing heart. Her prayers truly had been answered — and now she finally felt she could sleep for a solid week.

The next day even Marty was coaxed up on horseback in order to be given a tour of the ranch. She enjoyed the tiny flowers that nobly bloomed beside the trail, she thrilled to the sight of Willie's herds of cattle feeding on the hillsides, and she loved the placid mountains lined up against the sky in the distance. But she did *not* enjoy the wind sweeping across the prairie, pulling at her hair and skirt, nor the miles and miles of seeming emptiness. Marty watched Missie carefully as they rode together, and she could see in Missie's face that all she saw now was Willie's land as she had grown to love it.

Sunday arrived and with it some visitors to the LaHaye spread. At two o'clock in the afternoon, the opening hymn of their regular Sunday service was led by Henry Klein. Clark and Marty were happy to renew their acquaintance with the wagon driver who had come west with the LaHayes. Henry had changed much in those few short years. No longer a bashful, hesitant boy, he was now a sincere and confident man, presenting proudly an attractive wife and a two-year-old son, Caldwell.

As they sang the hymn, Marty glanced around her. Some of the LaHaye cowhands were there. She couldn't remember all the names, though she had been introduced. There was Cookie — she had no problem remembering Cookie — and Rusty and Lane. The other two names she could not recall. A neighborhood family had joined them for the service. Marty saw the small boy with the twisted arm, and her heart went out to him. These were the Newtons, a young couple with four young sons.

After the singing, Willie led the service and Clark was asked, as honored guest, to give the Bible lesson. The people were attentive, and Marty even heard an occasional quiet amen.

Juan and Maria and their baby girl and young son were not in attendance this time. Missie had told Marty about her friend and kept an eye on the road that twisted down the hill, no doubt hoping they would arrive, but when the service was over they still hadn't come. Missie was worried, she told her mother. It was the second Sunday in a row the de la Rosas had not showed up. They were not away from home, since Scottie had reported seeing them Friday. No one was ill, for they had all been in town together. Missie could not think of a reason for their absence, she explained, her voice low. She must call on them and see if there was some problem.

After the service ended, Missie served coffee and some of Wong's delicious doughnuts. They sat and visited, sharing their daily experiences, some joys and some difficulties. Marty and Clark were glad for the opportunity to get to know some of Missie and Willie's neighbors. They all seemed to feel that the service was a special time in their week.

The cowboys were the first to take their reluctant leave. It was time for their shift, and Scottie would be watching for them.

Next the Newtons also left. Mr. Newton as yet did not employ many hands on his spread and needed to get back in the saddle himself. He stated they hadn't been bothered much with rustlers lately, but one could never tell when they might decide to strike. The small, defenseless ranches were easy picking. The Newtons promised to be back again the next Sunday.

The Kleins stayed for supper. Marty could tell Wong was happy for the chance to show off his culinary skills. Nathan and Josiah, glad for a playmate, took Caldwell out to the patio to play with a delighted Max, who ran around in circles with excited yelps to remind them that for the last few days he had been getting very little attention.

Marty chatted with Melinda Klein while Missie fussed about the table, setting it with the good dishes and making sure everything looked its best. Marty soon came to feel very close to Melinda. Though some distance in age between them, they had shared similar experiences in their introduction to the West, both having lost a young husband in tragic accidents. Marty was glad that Melinda had Henry to help her over the hurt and confusion of losing the one she loved while so far away from friends and family. *And I'm glad I had Clark,* she thought with a quick glance at him across the room.

Henry, too, was anxious for news from the home area. Though Clark and Marty knew few of the people Henry would have claimed as neighbors, they were able to tell him some of the general news from the district.

Soon after the evening meal, the Kleins left for home and the boys were tucked in for the night. After their double portion of bedtime stories, they settled down, not to be heard from again till morning. Missie declared that the excitement of Sundays always tired them out.

Marty, too, felt tired, even though she was gradually catching up on the missed sleep. Willie informed her that it was the change in the altitude. Marty was willing to accept any excuse for her laziness. All she knew was that she was longing for her bed.

She hid a yawn and tried to get back into the conversation. Clark and Willie were making plans for the morning. It sounded as though wherever they were going, it would be a long ride. Willie was asking Missie if she wished to go. Marty was already stiff from her short ride of the day before. She wasn't sure she could handle another horseback ride, but Missie was answering, "I thought Mama and I should go on over to see Maria. I can't understand why they have missed two Sundays. If it's okay with Mama, we'll go and see what we can find out. I'm anxious for Mama and Maria to meet. You'll never believe Maria," Missie said, turning to Marty. "She speaks very good English now. Me — I hardly got a decent start on Spanish."

So it will be the saddle again tomorrow. Marty winced at the thought. Not only would she ride tomorrow, but from what she had understood, she would ride a long way. The de la Rosas were not *near* neighbors.

Marty nodded her head in agreement, hoping Missie did not read any hesitation.

Missie continued, "We should leave by nine. I think we'd better take the team so Mama won't need to ride so soon again, not being used to it. Besides, it's a fair ways and we'll need to take the boys. Could you have Scottie see that the team is ready for us, please?"

Willie nodded and Marty breathed in her relief. Everyone, now having settled on the plans for the morrow, decided that sleep would be needed to carry them through. They bade each other good-night and headed for their beds.

EIGHT
MARTY MEETS MARIA

The sun rose over the distant hills the next morning and right from the sunrise seemed to pour forth intense heat.

After breakfast and the morning chores, Willie brought the team around, and Missie loaded her sons and canteens with plenty of water for the day. Marty placed her bonnet firmly on her head as protection from the sun and wished she had a cooler gown.

"My, it's warm!" she exclaimed, but Missie did not seem bothered by the heat.

"A breeze should come up and cool things off some," she responded, then clucked to the team and they were off.

They had not gone far before Marty could feel the breeze, though she might have preferred to call it a gale. It was not anything like the cooling breezes that swept over the valley at home. In fact, Marty thought the wind felt even hotter than the sun. It whipped at her cheeks, drying and scorching them. It tore at her skirts and made the brim of her bonnet flap. Marty did not care for wind, and she wished it would blow elsewhere.

"I guess I've gotten used to the wind," Missie remarked as Marty tried to hold her bonnet down with one hand and her skirts with the other.

Nathan and Josiah rode comfortably on the first part of the journey, then began the age-old question, "How much longer?" Missie dealt with it good-naturedly until Nathan began to tease his younger brother, for lack of something else to do, and then she stopped the horses and lifted the youngsters down to stretch their legs. She gave them each a drink from a canteen and a couple of cookies and instructed them to play in the shade of the wagon while Mama and Grandma took a short walk. There was no shade for walking, so there was no temptation to linger. In fact, Marty was glad to be back in the wagon and moving again.

When they came to the river, Marty glanced up and down its length for a bridge. There was none. Missie confidently headed the horses into the stream, explaining as she did so that it used to flow deeper at that point until the men of the area widened the riverbed and allowed the stream to spread out. "Now," said Missie, "it's safe to cross here almost any time of year."

Marty, most relieved to hear it was safe, still gripped the wagon seat with white knuckles and snatched anxious glances over her shoulder at her grandsons. Crossing the river was the most exciting part of the journey for the boys. Marty heard their squeals of delight as the swirling water foamed about the wagon wheels. Once across, though, they began to coax their mother to hurry the team and complained they were too crowded, too hot, and too hungry.

Missie eventually handed the reins to Marty and took Josiah on her lap. Without Josiah to torment, Nathan, too, settled down for the remainder of the trip.

It was almost noon before the de la Rosas' buildings came into view. Marty saw a large, low ranch house, built of the same stone as Missie's home, though not quite as spacious. It nestled among brown hills, and there was not even a spring to add some green to the area. Missie informed Marty that the de la Rosas were fortunate in having all the water they needed from the deep well they had dug. The well now was showing its worth as a windmill turned busily in the ever-present wind, causing a pump to send a constant stream of water from its spout into a large animal trough.

"Well, it's nice to know thet the wind is good fer somethin'," murmured Marty under her breath as Missie guided the team into the yard and directed them to the hitching rail.

A young woman came rushing from the house.

"Missie!" she cried. "Oh, I'm so glad you have come. I've been missing our visits!" She saw Marty and stopped with embarrassment. "Oh, please do excuse my bad manners. I did not know that Missie was not alone. You must be the mother. The one Missie has missed and cried and prayed for."

Marty nodded and smiled.

"And I am Maria — the mindless one," she quipped. "I run heedless when I see a friend."

Marty laughed and extended her hand, then changed her mind and hugged Maria close.

"Missie has told me of ya," Marty said carefully. "Yer such a special friend, and I am so glad to meet ya," she finished warmly.

"And I you," said Maria, giving Marty a warm embrace in return, "though I must say that seeing you makes me even more longing for the mama of my own. It has been so long. . . ."

Maria did not finish her sentence. Missie had lifted the boys down, and they were clamoring for some attention.

"Where's José?" asked Nathan.

"He's in the house, where we all should be out of this hot sun. Come, you must get in out of the heat. You are brave to come on such a day." And Maria quickly led them all into her home.

"José is in the kitchen bothering the cook," she told Nathan. "You may get him and you can play in his room. I don't think that even our patient Carlos could put up with *two* small boys in the kitchen."

Nathan went to find José, and the ladies walked into the coolness of the sitting room, Josiah in tow. Marty felt so much better out of the sun. She slipped off her bonnet and was glad to wipe the perspiration from her face with a handkerchief. *My, it was a hot trip!*

Maria seated them and went for cool drinks. Upon hearing the two older boys chattering as they came from the kitchen, Josiah decided to tag along with them to José's room.

The ladies were left to sip cold tea and visit. The talk was centered around the family, area news, and ranching. Marty was included, though some of the phrases the two young women used regarding ranching were new to her.

"You should have waited for a day more less hot," said Maria and then laughed at her mixed-up English. "How you say it?" she asked Missie.

"A cooler day."

"My goodness — cooler, no! There is nothing cool about this day. How can it be more cool than something that is not cool at all?"

Marty and Missie laughed at Maria's reasoning. They had no answer to her logic.

"Anyway," said Maria, "it is very warm in the sun. We are used to it here, but you, Mrs. Davis, must find it bad to you."

"It is warm," admitted Marty. "This tea is jest right."

"Well, I guess we should have waited," Missie said. "But who knows, it might get hotter instead of cooler, and I did want to see you, Maria."

"A special reason?" asked Maria seriously.

"Rather special. We've been missing you on Sundays, and I was afraid — well, I wondered — that is, I hoped nothing was wrong."

At the mention of the Sunday service, Maria's head drooped.

"I wanted to go. I missed it. But Juan — well, he is not so sure. Not sure that we do the right thing. At home we teach our boy one thing — one way to pray, one way to worship God — and at the meeting, you teach him another way. It puzzles him. You understand? Juan, he thinks that we should not confuse our son with more than one God."

"But, Maria," exclaimed Missie, "we've talked about that! It's the same God. We worship the same God, just in a little different way."

"I know, I know," said Maria, her hands fluttering expressively. "I know all that. And I think that Juan, he even understands that. But he is frightened — frightened that José will not understand and he will not wish to worship God at all. Do you not see?"

"Yes, I see," said Missie slowly, tears filling her eyes. "I see."

"Oh, I am so glad. So glad that you understand. I was afraid you would not be able to see how we felt. I did not want you to think ill of me."

"Maria, I would never think ill of you."

Maria turned to hide her own tears. For a moment she couldn't speak, and then she turned back to her guests and the tears were running down her cheeks.

"You must pray for us. Right now Juan has many doubts, many questions. He cannot leave the church of his past, but he has here no church of his own. He does not want his child to grow up without the proper church teaching, but he is no longer sure what he wants our boy to be taught. There were things about Juan's church — actually, my church, too — that he did not agree with, but we love our church. Juan has not forsaken it. He will never forsake it. In the services at your house we have heard new and strange things from the Bible. We did not know of them before. It takes much wisdom, much time, much searching of the heart to know the truth. Please be patient with us, Missie. And please pray for us that we may know the truth. One day we think, 'This is it,' and the next day we say, 'No, that is it.' It is hard — so very hard."

"I understand," said Missie slowly. "We will pray. We will pray that you will find the truth — not that you will believe as we believe, but that you will find the truth. We believe with all our heart that God has given His truth to us in His Son Jesus Christ, that He came to die for us and to forgive us our sins, and —" Missie stopped short. "But you believe that, too, Maria. You have told me that Jesus is the only way that one can come to God."

"Oh yes," said Maria. "That is the truth."

"Then all we really need to pray about is that God will show you and Juan if it's all right to worship with us."

"I . . . I think so. We have been taught one way — you another."

"We will continue to pray."

"It is so important to Juan to raise his children in the correct way. You see, his family —" But Maria stopped midsentence and hastened to her feet. "I must see if Carlos has our coffee and cakes ready. You will have cooled enough by now to be able to enjoy some of Carlos's coffee." She hurried away without waiting for a reply.

The talk over the coffee turned to lighter matters. They chatted about new material, dress patterns, and the gardens that were growing daily in spite of the heat. Missie finally announced that they must go, and Maria sent José and Nathan to find Pedro, the yard hand, to bring the team and hitch up the wagon.

While the boys were running off to find the old man and give him the message, the women prepared to leave.

"Please," said Maria, "please could we have a prayer together? I have missed it so."

They knelt to pray. Missie prayed first,

followed by Marty, and then it was Maria's turn. She began slowly, in carefully chosen English, and then she stopped and turned to the other two ladies. "Do you mind — will you excuse me — if I talk to God in my own language? I know He understands my heart in any language, but I think He understands *my* tongue better in the language of my birth." At their nods and smiles, Maria continued her prayer. Never had Marty heard a more fervent one. Maria poured out her soul to her God in honey-flowing Spanish. Though Marty could not understand a word of it, she understood the spirit of the prayer, and her heart prayed along with Maria. Surely God would answer this young woman's yearning for the truth.

NINE
THE RESCUE

Though still too warm for Marty's liking, the weather turned a bit more bearable. Missie and Marty kept close to the shelter of the house, but Clark rode with the men almost daily. Marty could tell his farmer's heart responded to the wide expanse of hillsides and roaming cattle, and he declared many times his love of the mountains.

Nathan clamored for his grandfather's attention. He was anxious to show off "his" part of the ranch to Clark. As yet, he was not allowed to roam freely on the open range. But there were well-worn trails closer to home that he claimed as his own. He had ridden them since he had been a baby carried on his mother's back. Now Josiah had replaced Nathan on Missie's horse, and Nathan was allowed the privilege of his own pony.

"Could ya ride with me today, Grandpa?" Nathan begged at the breakfast table.

"Well, I shore don't see why not," answered Clark. "I 'spect maybe yer pa will be able to git by without me fer this here one day."

Nathan took his grandfather's words seriously. "Ya can help him again tomorra," he assured Clark, causing laughter to ripple around the table.

"An' where're we ridin' today?"

"I'll show ya the west ridge."

"An' are there lots of excitin' things to see on the west ridge?"

Nathan nodded his head vigorously, since his mouth was too full of scrambled eggs to speak.

"Well, then," said Clark, "why don't we jest go on out fer a look-see?"

Nathan's eyes sparkled in anticipation. He hurried through his meal and bounced down from the table.

"What horse shall I tell Scottie to saddle for ya, Grandpa?" he asked with excitement.

"Nathan," said Willie quietly, indicating Nathan's empty chair.

Nathan crawled back up reluctantly and looked over at his mother, then back at his father. "May I be excused, sir?" he asked, subdued.

Willie nodded and Nathan swung down from the chair.

"What horse —" he began, but Clark stopped him with a laugh.

"I think Scottie's busy enough without worryin' none 'bout me. I'll saddle ol' Turk when I git down there."

Nathan spun around and was gone. "I'll get Spider," he called over his shoulder as he ran out the door, then followed it with, "Too bad Joey's too little."

"Joey?" questioned Marty.

Missie laughed. "I thought and thought of a name for my second son that wouldn't be all chopped up in a nickname. I thought I had one, too. Josiah. Surely no one could shorten that. But I wasn't counting on Nathan. He's called him Joey since the day he arrived."

"I think it's rather nice," Marty mused.

"Well, I guess it's all right — you know what I've decided? I've decided that almost any name is all right as long as it's spoken with love."

Marty smiled her agreement.

Clark finished his coffee and turned to Willie. "Well, cowboy, it looks like you'll jest have to do yer best wranglin' without me today. I've got me another pardner."

Willie grinned. "Wish I could come with ya, but I promised Hugh Caly thet I'd ride on over and take a look at some new stock he brought in. Yer lucky to be missin' thet ride. It's a long, hot one, an' to save some miles, we pass right through some bad cactus territory. Near scratches the clothes right off ya."

"Thet there west ridge sounds better 'n better to me." Clark smiled.

"Nothing much of danger on the west ridge. Thet's why we allow Nathan to ride there. Pretty lifeless over there. Ya'll be lucky to even spy a rattler slitherin' off."

"Well, iffen there be a rattler, I do hope it slithers off, all right," said Clark. "I haven't grown overfond of 'em."

"Jest don't surprise 'em," said Willie, "an' you'll be all right."

When Clark reached the barn, Scottie was unobtrusively giving Nathan a hand with the saddling of Spider. Clark went into the corral to bring out Turk. He still wasn't too handy with the rope, but he managed to get the horse on the second try.

They saddled up and left the yard, Missie calling to them as they rode out to make sure they both had full canteens.

"Ma always worries," confided Nathan in a loud whisper, to which Clark responded, "Thet's what mas are for."

They rode to the west, then turned toward the south and followed the ridge for a few miles. There really wasn't much new to see but an occasional glimpse of the mountain chain as it topped one of the nearer hills. Often they could look out to the east and see cattle, as Willie's herd fed its way across the prairie. Once or twice they spotted a cowboy as he hazed the cattle. The sun was high in the sky when Clark suggested they pull over in the shelter of some big rocks and eat the lunch Missie had sent along. Nathan seemed to like the idea. The eating time was the most important part of any trail ride. Nathan crawled down from Spider and ground-tied him. Clark did likewise with Turk, looking around cautiously to make sure there were no rattlers sharing the rocks with them. He noticed Nathan doing likewise.

"If rattlers are here, Grandpa, they'll be in the sun 'stead of on this shady side," he said. "But still Pa says ya always got to check to be sure."

Clark was pleased with the boy's knowledge of his environment and his carefulness.

"How much further we goin'?" asked Clark as they munched their sandwiches.

"Not much, I guess. Nothin' to see down there 'cept some ol' hills with holes in 'em."

"Ol' hills with holes?"

Nathan nodded.

"What kind of holes?"

"Pa says they used to mine it."

"Mine it?"

"Yeah."

"What kind of mine?"

"Dunno. Pa says fer me to stay away from the holes. He says they are dang'rous. Some stuff is gittin' rotten or somethin'."

"Best we stay away from 'em, then," agreed Clark, but he planned on asking Willie about the old mines when he got home.

They had just finished their lunch and were gathering things together when they heard an approaching horse. The rider was coming full gallop, and Clark stood up to see what the reason might be. One did not usually ride at such pace in the heat of the midday sun.

A young rider approached them, his legs beating at the sides of his horse and his unruly hair flying in the wind. Clark could hear him shout now and then, but he couldn't understand a word he was saying.

"Who's thet?" Clark asked the young Nathan.

For a moment Nathan just stood and stared without answering.

"Who is he? Ya know?" Clark asked again.

Nathan roused then, shaking his head.

The rider pounded closer, and Clark could plainly hear him sobbing now. Clark stepped forward to be ready to stop the horse when the boy drew near.

"You gotta come!" the frantic boy screamed even before he reached them. "You gotta come quick! Andy and Abe, they —"

He had reached them, and Clark hauled in the lathered horse.

"Whoa, there," he said, reaching up in one smooth movement both to pull the horse to a halt and to run a quieting hand over its neck.

"You gotta come —" The boy's voice was agitated and hoarse with emotion.

Clark moved a hand to the boy. "Jest take it easy. Take it easy. We'll come. Now ya calm down some 'n' tell —"

"Abe an' Andy!" cried the boy, tears making tracks down his dust-covered cheeks. "Abe an' Andy are in there."

"Take it easy," Clark said again. "Jest tell it slow like."

"We gotta hurry!" the boy barked impatiently.

"We'll hurry," said Clark. "But first we gotta know where to hurry to." Clark's purposeful calm seemed to have its effect, and the boy took a big breath before continuing.

"The mine. The ol' mine shaft — they're in there. It fell on 'em. They'll never git out."

"Where?"

"Over there. We were lookin' 'em over, an' the timbers broke an' the mine fell in —"

But Clark was already gathering the reins of his horse. "Nathan," he said, "can ya ride home alone? Does yer pa ever let ya do thet?"

"Sure," said Nathan, his eyes wide.

"Look, son," said Clark, pulling the boy close. "I want ya to ride on back to the ranch. Tell Scottie, or whoever is around, thet some boys are trapped in a mine. Tell 'em to bring shovels an' a wagon an' come on the double. Ya got thet?"

Nathan nodded his head in agreement, his eyes wide with the importance of his mission.

"Now ya ride on home. Take yer time — do ya hear? Don't try to go fast. Jest take yer time an' be careful. I'm gonna go with this here boy an' help those kids. All right?"

Clark boosted Nathan onto his pony and watched as the small boy headed back to the ranch on the familiar path. He was not concerned about the boy becoming lost. Nathan knew the way well. Clark was worried that panic might cause him to travel too fast and maybe end up in a spill. Nathan turned once to look back at his grandfather. "Remember. Go slow," Clark called to him, and the boy waved his hand.

The sobbing of the boy beside him brought Clark's head around.

"Okay, son. You lead the way. Take it easy. A fall with yer horse won't help yer friends none."

They started for the mine, the boy's spent horse wheezing for breath in choking gasps. Clark found that the mine was farther away than he had first thought.

The boy still wept sporadically. He pushed his horse as fast as the poor creature could go. When they finally reached an opening in the side of a hill, he threw himself off.

"They're in there!" he cried. "We gotta git 'em out."

Smoke-colored dust still lingered in the air, evidence of a recent cave-in.

"You know this mine?" he asked the boy.

"Some," the boy admitted with downcast eyes, and Clark could see that he knew it was forbidden territory.

Some boards that obviously had closed off the cave entrance had been pried off and discarded at the side of its open mouth.

"Tell me 'bout it," Clark said, and as the

boy hesitated, Clark took his arm. "Yer friends are in there. Remember? Now, I don't know one thing about thet there cave. Tell me 'bout it. Does it have more than one branch? How far back were ya? Did the timbers collapse more'n once?"

The boy responded. "It has three main tunnels. The first one takes off real quick to the right. It's a short one. Don't think the miners found anything there, so they jest left it. The second one goes off to the right, too. But the fellas are in the left one. It's the biggest an' was used the most. The timbers're really bad in there. The shaft goes down deeper in the left one. Sometimes the steps are real steep an' slippery. We was climbin' up an' we kept slippin', so we grabbed hold of the side timbers to pull ourselves, an' thet's when it . . ." He couldn't continue but put his face in his hands and sobbed.

Clark stayed long enough to hold him for a moment. "It's okay. We'll git 'em. Are there any shovels?"

The boy shook his head. "We can use our hands," he snuffled.

"Yer not comin' back in," said Clark, seeing the terror in the boy's face.

"But I gotta," he said through sobs. "I gotta."

"No, yer needed here. They're gonna come from the ranch. Ya need to tell 'em where to go. They'll have shovels. Ya tell 'em, too, 'bout those rotten timbers. Ya hear?"

The boy nodded. Clark hoped the youth would be able to wait calmly without further panic.

Clark gently pushed him to a sitting position on a nearby rock. "Ya jest stay right there an' wait fer those men. Now, it might seem a long time till they come, but they'll be here. Ya jest keep watchin' fer 'em an' wave 'em on over here. Ya okay now?"

The boy nodded again, affirming that he was. His face was still white beneath the smears of dust and tears.

Clark turned and headed for the mine. The door was low, and he had to stoop to enter. Old beams above his head appeared as his eyes adjusted to the dimness. The supports looked fairly stable in some places and sagging and broken in others. Clark moved away from the light at the entrance and felt his way along the passage. He had not gone far when he found the first tunnel off to the right just as the boy had described. He continued on, feeling his way with his hands and his feet. A low-hanging beam caught him by surprise, and he banged his head against the knotted lumber. For a minute he felt dizzy with the pain, but he steadied himself until he had his bearings. From then on he went forward with one arm outstretched above his head.

Clark ducked his way past other obstructions. How he wished for a light. He figured the boys must have used some kind of torches or lanterns to find their way around. Clark discovered the second right-hand tunnel. *Only one more to go,* he told himself. The tunnel should soon swing to the left. After several yards of total darkness, Clark felt the tunnel veer sharply. The smell of dust was heavy in the air now. Clark was forced to stop and tie his handkerchief over his nose. He started down the left fork and soon came to one of the steep places the boy had described. Before he knew what was happening, his feet had slipped out from under him, and he felt himself sliding downward on his back. The rocks cut into him, scraping away shirt and skin. After he had come to a halt and felt cautiously about, Clark regained his feet and pressed slowly forward, testing carefully with his foot before he put his weight on it. Again and again the tunnel took a downward turn, but Clark was ready for them, most only a step or two. And then, just ahead of him,

Clark thought he heard a groan. He fell to his hands and knees and felt his way forward.

"Hello," he called. "Hello. Do you hear me? Hello."

Another groan answered him, and Clark crawled on.

Soon he was in contact with a slight body. "Do you hear me?" he asked, reaching for the boy's wrist and the pulse. The boy stirred. Clark felt a faint pulse beat and breathed a prayer of thanks.

"Son," he asked anxiously, "son. Can you hear me? Are ya awake?"

In answer the boy began to cry. "Ya came," he sobbed. "Ya came."

"It's all right." Clark soothed him, brushing his hair back out of his face and feeling the dirt and debris falling off his head. "It's all right. Where are ya hurt? Can ya get up?"

"My ankle," sobbed the boy. "It's caught under thet beam."

"We'll git it out. We'll have it out in no time. Ya jest hang in there."

"Abe," said the boy. "Did ya git Abe yet?"

"Not yet," answered Clark.

Clark began to feel around in the darkness. He had to discover just what was holding the boy's leg. He found the beam, a big piece of timber, too thick and too long for him to tackle without some kind of tool.

He went on searching, feeling his way in search of the other boy. Carefully he made his way over the rubble and back again, the sharp stones cutting into the flesh of his palms. Nothing. He crawled on. He nearly missed it, but just as his hand slid over some rocky debris, he felt something smooth to the touch. It was a boot. Clark allowed his hand to search out the area. The boy was almost totally buried under the cave-in. Clark began to dig away at the rock and dirt, trying not to dislodge any more of the tunnel wall in his haste.

At length he could feel an arm. He dug on, frantically searching out the place where the head might be, eventually uncovering it. He longed for a light. If only he could see the condition of the boy. His hands traced over the temple, the face, the back of the head, and back again. They told him all that he needed to know. Clark crawled back to Andy.

"Andy," he said. "Andy. Ya still with me, boy?"

The boy groaned his answer.

"Andy, I've gotta try to git yer leg out. Now, I can't move thet there beam. It's too big an' heavy an' I don't have anything to cut it with. I'm gonna have to try to dig out from under yer leg and git it out thet way. It's gonna hurt, Andy. Can ya take it?"

Andy was crying again. "Yeah," he said. "We gotta git out. These timbers keep creakin' like they're gonna break again."

Clark crawled around, feeling for a sharp rock. He found one he thought would make a tool of sorts and began to dig around the boy's leg. At first he worked far enough away from the boy that the digging did not bother him, but as the rubble was gradually cleared away, the leg began to shift and the boy moaned in pain. This turned into a tortured scream, but Clark dug on, trying his hardest to be as gentle as he knew how. He must get him out, and quickly, for the boy was right. Clark, too, could hear the timbers snapping and creaking and feared at any time they might give way and pour forth more rocks and earth on top of them.

It seemed forever to Clark until he had a hole clawed away beneath Andy's foot deep enough to coax the boy's ankle out. He would have to slip off the boot in order to make the foot squeeze under. Pulling off the boot made Andy scream again in pain. Clark almost succumbed to the cries and stopped twisting, but he knew he would be signing the boy's life away if he did. He had dug away the earth to sheer rock. He could make the opening no bigger for the injured ankle to pass through. If Andy was to be freed, he must pull him loose now. Clark gritted his teeth, took the foot as gently as he could, and forced the leg out from under the beam. Mercifully, Andy fainted. Clark wiped dirt from the boy's face and loosened his collar. Then he picked him up gently and started carefully back up the tunnel.

Stumbling along in the darkness, feeling his way with an outstretched toe, bumping against rocks and beams that obstructed the path was treacherous going. The steep incline was the most difficult. One time he had to slide the boy up ahead of him, then claw his way up behind him and go on again. On and on he stumbled and fought until at least he could sense, more than see, the tunnel to his right. He breathed a thanksgiving prayer and hurried on. The tunnel floor was smoother now and walking was easier. Soon Clark passed the second tunnel, as well. If only the men from the ranch would be there with a light and some shovels.

And then, just ahead, Clark saw the opening of the mine. He hastened forward and burst out to fresh air and glaring sunshine. The boy was sitting in the shade on the same rock where Clark had seated him. He sprang to his feet when Clark made an appearance.

"Ya found Andy!" he cried. "Andy. Andy, ya okay?" He was crying again. "Is he dead, mister?"

"Naw," said Clark. "He's okay. He's got a busted ankle, but he'll be okay. Run over there to my saddle an' git thet there canteen. He needs a drink." The boy ran away in a flash.

Clark laid the boy gently on the ground in the shade. He stood to full height and looked off in the direction of the ranch. In the distance he could see whirls of dust. They were on their way. He couldn't wait. The timbers might give way at any moment and then the other boy, Abe, would be buried deep within the mine shaft.

He turned to the boy who was kneeling beside his friend Andy, trying to help him with a few swallows of water.

"Listen," he said. "They are on their way here now. See thet dust over there? It's gonna take 'em a while to git here. I want ya to take good care of Andy till they come, an' when they git here you just tell 'em to wait out here fer me. Ya understand? I know where Abe is, an' I'm gonna go git 'im."

The boy nodded his head and Clark turned and hurried back into the old mine.

Traveling more quickly this time with a better idea of what was ahead of him, he still protected himself with a raised arm and a groping foot. But he moved with less caution because he knew that time was a major factor.

As he felt and slipped his way down the left tunnel, he prayed that he might get to Abe before the whole mine collapsed. The dust still hung heavily in the air, but Clark didn't think it was any worse than before. It appeared there had been no further cave-ins.

He came to the last steep slide and let himself down carefully, trying hard not to disturb any more of the rock around him. At the bottom, he dropped on all fours and felt his way forward to where he had left Abe. In the darkness he found the outstretched arm and the near-buried face, and he began to dig methodically, painstakingly, lifting away the debris from around him. It was slow work. Some of the rocks that buried the boy were boulder sized, and it took all of Clark's strength to move them to the side. He clawed and pushed, pulled and scratched, tore and pried until at last he had the boy freed from his prison.

He stopped for only a minute to catch his breath, and then he lifted the boy tenderly and once again began the climb to the outside world. Just as he pushed Abe ahead of him up the steep slope, there was a terrifying crack and a monstrous roar, and the ceiling of the cavern collapsed all around him. Pain seared through Clark as a heavy timber fell with sickening impact upon his leg, and then merciful blackness.

The men in the wagon had just pulled up and began to throw questions at the boy when the roar from within the cave burst upon them. Another cave-in! The boy crumpled to the ground with a cry of despair, and Andy, who lay on the ground shivering in shock, began to whimper.

"Someone look after thet boy," barked Scottie, and Lane moved forward to examine the youngster and ordered some blankets brought from the wagon.

Willie headed for the mine entrance and was stopped by Scottie's hands.

"I'm goin' in," Willie told his foreman.

"No, ya ain't. Nobody's goin' in there till we know thet it's finished fallin'."

Willie hesitated and stood listening to the rumbling inside the hillside.

The dust began to sift out of the entrance as they stood and stared, straining their ears. Willie turned to the sobbing boy.

"Did the man who came with ya go in there, boy?"

The boy nodded his head.

"Has he been out a'tall?"

"He brought Andy out."

"Where is he now?"

"He went back in fer Abe."

It was exactly as Willie knew it would be, yet he had dared to hope it might not be so.

The rumbling gradually stopped. Willie headed for the wagon and came back with a lantern and a rope. Again Scottie stepped forward and without a word took the lantern from him and lit it.

"Lane," Scottie instructed, "grab these shovels an' follow me."

Willie moved to fall in line.

"Mr. LaHaye," said Scottie, "you ain't goin' in there."

"What ya talkin' —" Willie began, but Scottie interrupted.

"I'm talkin' 'bout *you*," said Scottie firmly. "You an' yer missus an' those two little boys."

"But —"

"No buts. Thet there mine might *give* again. Ya know thet, an' I know thet."

Scottie then turned to Lane. "I'm not askin' any man to take chances," he said. "You stay several feet behind me an' iffen

154

ya hear a rumble, then run fer it. Now, boy, where do we find 'em?"

The youngster moved forward and was able to again intelligently give the men directions, and then Scottie and Lane moved through the mine opening.

Willie fidgeted at the entry. He wanted to go in and help with the search for Clark. He *would* go in. And then he thought of Missie. Of Missie and his two sons. If anything should happen to her father, she would need her husband even more.

Praying, he paced back and forth before the mouth of the mine and then went over to see if there was anything he could do for the young boy who lay groaning on the ground.

He turned to the one who leaned against the rock outcropping, staring at the gaping hole that had caused all this misery.

"Boy," he said, "do ya live 'round here?"

"In town," he answered.

"This yer brother?" asked Willie, indicating Andy on the ground.

"My friend. My brother — he's still in there."

"Yer folks be worryin'?"

"I reckon."

"Do ya think ya should ride on home an' tell 'em? Yer pa might want to git on over here an' help git yer brother out."

The boy looked surprised that he hadn't thought of that.

"Yeah," he said and headed for his grazing horse.

"An' git word to the folks of this here boy, too, will ya, son? They can come over and see what they can do to make 'im more comfortable."

The boy cast a backward glance at his friend and hurried off.

From then on, there was nothing for Willie to do except watch the entrance of the mine and pray there would be no more cave-ins. Occasionally he talked to the half-conscious boy or gave him sips of water. The broken ankle was painful, but as Willie examined it with his eyes, not wanting to move it, he thought it looked as though it might heal properly. He could see no protruding bones or broken skin.

There was nothing to speed up the minutes as Willie waited. Time after time he started down the mine tunnel, only to think of Scottie's words and turn back.

After what seemed like an eternity, another wagon pulled up. A man whom Willie had seen only once before jumped to the ground before the wagon even stopped rolling. He stopped briefly to touch the face of Andy and give a brief nod to Willie, and then he ran into the entrance of the mine. He did not even carry a lantern.

A woman approached more slowly. Already her face was tear-streaked and her eyes swollen from weeping.

"Is this yer son?" asked Willie with concern in his voice.

The woman knelt beside the boy and smoothed his hair with her hand and wiped the dust from his face with an edge of her simple gown.

"No," she said, her voice trembling. "It's my boy still in there."

"I'm sorry," said Willie.

"We've told 'em — over an' over we've warned 'em. 'Don't go near those mines,' we've said. 'They're not safe.' But bein' boys they jest gotta find out fer theirselves." She was sobbing softly, not bothering with the tears that ran down her cheeks.

"Somebody should do something 'bout those caves," the woman went on. "Ya never know whose child might be next."

Willie thought of his own two boys. "We'll git a permit to dynamite 'em, ma'am, jest as soon as we git these folks out."

The boy stirred and the woman spoke to him. "It's okay, Andy. Casey has gone fer yer ma an' pa. They should be here anytime now. They'll git ya on home an' look to thet ankle."

Andy, looking relieved in spite of his pain, closed his eyes again.

Willie scanned the hills once more and could see another wagon approaching in the distance. It was not long until Andy's folks arrived and the mother was running to him with shrieks and cries. Willie feared she was going to turn hysterical, but her husband calmed her. She fell on the ground beside her son and alternated between scoldings and endearments. The man knelt over the foot and began to prod the ankle. The boy cried out in pain, and the father grimaced and then went about preparing a makeshift splint. It was not a pleasant task. The boy screamed again and again as the foot was placed at the right angle and bound. Everyone present had broken into a cold sweat before the ordeal was over. At length the father's gruesome task was done, and he buried his face in his hands and sobbed. And still there was no sign of life from the mouth of the mine.

"How long they been in there?" asked one of the mothers.

"I've long since lost track of time," answered Willie. "Seems forever. At least there's been no more rumbles. Thet's a good sign."

He paced back and forth and again ventured into the cave a short distance. Then he heard the scraping and sliding of scuffling feet, and as he strained forward he could see the faint light of a lantern reflecting off the tunnel wall.

He pushed forward more anxiously and soon was face-to-face with Scottie. Scottie carried the front end of a makeshift stretcher made from broken timbers, and Lane stumbled along behind carrying the other end. On the stretcher lay Clark. His face was deathly white and blood smeared, and the arm that dangled at his side swung lifelessly back and forth.

"Oh, dear God," prayed Willie, and then to the men, "Is he dead?"

Scottie did not answer. Lane finally dared to voice a quiet "Not quite."

Willie took the lantern that swung from one corner of the stretcher and led the way. As he turned to check on the progress of the men behind him, he noticed the third man. It was the boy's father, and he, too, bore a burden. In his arms he carried his boy. Willie's eyes asked the question, and this time Scottie answered. "No" was all he said.

TEN
A DAY OF A MILLION YEARS

They took Clark to the ranch on a makeshift bed in the wagon. Even in his unconscious state, he groaned occasionally. They tried to drive as carefully as they could, but the jarring vehicle was distressful at best and a torment at worst.

Scottie guided the team, turning this way and that as he snaked a pathway home, trying his best to miss chuckholes and bumps. Willie sat with Clark, steadying him and bathing his face with water from the canteen. Except for the lump on his head from the falling beam and the badly injured leg, Clark seemed to have no other wounds. Willie dared to hope that the head injury would be a mild concussion, that Clark's mind would not suffer any serious effects from it.

The leg was another matter. As Willie looked at the severely broken leg with the bone splinter projecting from the skin, he shuddered. How could such a leg heal without the help of a doctor? "Oh, dear God," prayed Willie aloud, "please show us what to do."

As the wagon neared the ranch, an anxious Marty and Missie hurried out into the yard. Willie chided himself for not thinking to go ahead and prepare his womenfolk, and he jumped from the slow-moving wagon and asked Lane to watch Clark, and Scottie to drive as slowly as he knew how. Then Willie quickened his stride and reached the women slightly ahead of the wagon.

"Clark been hurt?" gasped Marty.

Willie nodded.

"Bad?" cried Missie.

"Pretty bad," answered Willie, "but not as bad as it will seem at first. He took a knock on the head, so he ain't conscious jest yet."

"Oh, dear God," whispered Marty, her hand fluttering to her throat, but Willie thought he saw relief showing in her eyes that at least Clark was alive.

"Did ya git the boys?"

"Yes," Willie nodded.

"Thank God," breathed Marty.

Just before the wagon rolled up, Willie placed an arm around each of the women. He wanted just another minute to prepare them.

"Yer pa also has a broken leg," he said to Missie. "We'll need to fix his bed right away. Then fetch some hot water and towels from the kitchen. We want to move him as gentle as we can. Will ya see to it? An', Ma, could ya check to see what we might have around in the way of disinfectant — he's got some scratches we should look after."

With a quick glance toward the now-stopped wagon, the two women ran toward the house to do Willie's bidding.

Willie moved forward.

"Quick," he said to Scottie. "I want him in there an' settled 'fore the women . . ." He did not finish. He did not need to. Scottie understood. Lane rushed out to help them, and with the three men manning the makeshift bed, they got Clark to the house. Missie had already turned down the bed in readiness, but just as Willie had hoped, neither of the women were in the room.

The men laid Clark on the bed and removed his shirt. Willie found some scissors and cut the pant leg from the broken limb. Scottie had removed the shoes and socks.

"We should bundle him warm against shock," said Lane, and Willie reached for a flannel nightshirt, which they struggled to slip over Clark's head.

"What we gonna do about thet leg?" It

was a question they no doubt had all been asking themselves, but it was Lane who finally voiced it.

"For now we'll jest protect it all we can an' let the women see him fer a minute," Willie said.

Marty was the first one through the door. She cried out at the sight of Clark and went to kneel beside him, brushing at the dirt streaks and bloodstains on his pale face and running her fingers through his hair. Willie remained silent for a few minutes and then asked quietly, "Did ya find some disinfectant?"

Marty held up the forgotten bottle with trembling fingers.

Missie arrived with a basin of hot water and some towels. Willie took them from her and she rushed forward to kneel by her mother. She lifted one of Clark's limp hands and began to stroke it, as if willing it to become strong and independent again.

Willie remained silent for a moment and then passed Marty a small towel.

"Ya want to clean up his face some? Make sure the water isn't too hot. He won't be able to warn ya, and we don't want a burn."

Marty and Missie both came to life then.

"I'll go fetch a pitcher of cool water," said Missie and fled from the room. Marty turned to the business of cleaning Clark up. She inspected his dirty blood-caked hands, exclaiming over the bruised knuckles and the scratched and dirt-stained palms. His nails were broken and dirt filled from digging with his fingers.

"My, but they're a mess," said Marty, new calmness in her voice as she set about her task.

Willie sighed with relief and lifted the basin from the nearby chest so Missie could add the cold water she had just brought into the room.

The two women soaked and cleansed the damaged hands and then applied the disinfectant that Marty had produced. They wiped his face and found that, except for a couple of minor scratches, there were no open wounds there. Clark did not stir. Willie observed Marty slyly feeling for a pulse and looking relieved when she actually found one. After Willie was sure the women had spent enough time with Clark to reassure them, he turned to Missie. "I'm gonna have to ask ya fer a favor now. I know it'll be hard to leave yer pa, but I do need to ask ya to care fer a few things fer me."

Missie's eyes widened, but she nodded in agreement.

"Some of the boys were out there diggin'

most of the afternoon. They're hungry an' Cookie's already cleared away from the last meal. Could you rustle up a bunch of sandwiches an' some hot coffee fer 'em?"

Missie, surprised, hesitated only a moment. She had never been asked to fix anything for the ranch hands before. Cookie always took care of their food needs no matter what time they came in. But she did not question Willie, only moved to obey.

"Do ya mind givin' her a hand?" Willie asked Marty.

Marty was about to protest and then rose to her feet. Surely this small request was not too much for Willie to ask.

"The boys have a shift change soon an' gotta git on out to the cattle," Willie went on quickly with his explanation.

He was relieved when Marty nodded and moved from the room. Willie immediately left the room and went to the boys' room. Josiah was napping and Nathan was playing quietly. Missie had asked him to go to his room before Clark was carried into the house so the small boy would not be unduly frightened by his grandfather's condition.

"Hi, fella," greeted Willie as cheerily as the occasion would allow him. "Would ya mind doin' a little chore fer yer pa?"

"Mama said thet I was to stay here till she

came for me," answered Nathan. And then in deep seriousness, he went on, "Did Grandpa git the boys out, Pa?"

"He sure 'nough did," answered Willie, roughing the boy's hair. "But I need ya now. I'll tell yer ma thet I had a job fer ya. I want ya to run real quick an' tell Cookie an' Scottie thet I need 'em at the house. Tell 'em I need 'em *now*. Then come right back here to yer room. Okay?"

Nathan laid aside his book and ran as his pa bade him. Scottie and Cookie quickly arrived at Clark's room.

"Quick," said Willie. "I've got the ladies busy in the kitchen fixin' a lunch fer the hands."

"Lunch fer the hands?" repeated Cookie in disbelief.

"It was all I could think of to git 'em from the room. Now we gotta clean up thet leg, an' we gotta do it quick like."

The two men nodded and Willie threw back the blankets. The sight that met their gaze was not a pleasant one. For a moment, Willie wished he could just throw the blanket over the leg again and walk away.

Cookie forgot himself and swore under his breath. " 'Bout the worst one I ever seed," he said. "Even worse shape than my hip was."

"Well, we gotta do what we can. Pass thet there basin." The three men worked over the wound, soaking and cleaning it and then pouring on the whole bottle of disinfectant. Willie tried to straighten the leg so that it didn't lie at such a bizarre angle, but they knew there was nothing they could do to set the bone. After the thorough cleansing, they fixed a loose makeshift splint and wrapped the damaged leg in it, more to conceal the injury than to do it any good. They were just finishing when Willie heard Missie's quick, light step.

"Thet lunch'll be ready soon," he whispered to the other two. "Ya go on out an' find someone — anyone — to eat it."

Cookie nodded and went out to round up some cowboys. Scottie, at a nod from his boss, also left the room. Willie heard him speak to Missie in the hall.

"I hear tell thet ya're gonna fix some sandwiches, ma'am. I'll jest wash some of the dirt off me at the cook shack an' I'll be right in. Mighty nice of ya, an' I sure am in need of a cup of coffee. Mighty obliged, ma'am."

Willie covered Clark carefully and picked up the basin with the dirty, bloody water. He held it up high so Missie couldn't see into it.

"Yer pa seems to be restin' a mite easier now," he said, backing out of the room with his rather gruesome-looking burden. "Thanks fer feedin' the men, Missie. Ya might tell yer ma thet if she wishes to sit with yer pa, the fellas can care fer themselves in the kitchen. An', Missie, I think thet Nathan might need a little reassurance. He must be wonderin' jest what's goin' on. I sent him on a little chore fer me, an' he was 'fraid you'd scold him fer leavin' his room unbidden. Ya might like to peek in and sorta calm him some. I gotta run. Gotta make a little trip. Won't be long."

Missie looked dumbfounded at Willie's announcement, but she nodded mutely and moved toward the boys' room. Willie ached to hold her for a minute, but his hands were occupied with the basin and dirty towels. He sensed that his wife was probably still in shock.

"Missie," he said softly and she turned back, "he's gonna be all right. He's tough. As soon as thet little bump on his head . . ." His voice trailed off. Then he went on. "Tell yer ma not to let him move. Iffen he wakes up an' thrashes 'round, call fer Scottie. We couldn't set thet there leg yet, an' he might hurt himself."

Again Missie nodded silent assent. Willie

moved on by her with the basin.

"An', Missie. Try not to worry. I'll be back as soon as I can."

He passed through the door and headed for the bunkhouse and cook shack. He tossed the dirty water to the side of the path. When he reached the shack he found Cookie.

"Could only find three riders," said Cookie, "an' even they weren't hungry. Told 'em to eat or else."

"Lane an' Scottie should be hungry," said Willie. "They ain't had anythin' since —"

"This sort of thing takes one's appetite," answered Cookie. "But they'll eat. They'll eat all right, an' they'll drink the coffee. They need the coffee."

Willie passed Cookie the blood-soaked towels. "Think thet ya can clean 'em up some 'fore the womenfolk see 'em again?"

"Shore," said Cookie and tossed them in a corner.

"Tell Scottie I had to go into town. Tell 'im I want an eye kept on thet house. Iffen those women need help, I want someone to be there."

Cookie said nothing, but his eyes assured Willie that the order would be followed.

Willie strode on down to the corral, where he lifted a rope from a post and snaked out his saddle horse. In a few minutes' time the sound of pounding hoofbeats was echoing across the yard.

Marty had had a hard time concentrating on fixing a lunch for the men with Clark lying in the bedroom in his present condition. She couldn't remember how many scoops of coffee to put into the pot, nor could she remember where to find bread and butter. Missie's memory didn't seem much better, even if it was her own kitchen. Wong was down in the garden selecting vegetables for supper, and neither of the women thought to call him.

Numbly they went about searching out sandwich materials and spreading the bread. Neither talked, although both were aware of anxious thoughts that would not be stilled. They worked on in silence until Marty noticed Missie fighting back the tears. She went to her then and took her in her arms.

"He'll be all right. God won't let anythin' happen to 'im. He'll be fine." Oh, how Marty wanted to believe her own words! *They have to be true. They just have to. If anything happens to Clark . . .* Her arms tightened around Missie and she began to pray aloud.

"God, ya know how we need ya now. Ya know how we love Clark. Ya know how he has served you. He loves ya, Lord. An' now we're askin' thet ya lift him up. Thet ya give 'im back his mind an' body, iffen it be yer will, Lord. Amen."

Missie looked at Marty, her eyes wide and the tears streaming down her face. "Oh, Ma," she cried, "don't pray like that! *Of course* it is His will. Of course it is. He *must* heal him. He must."

Marty, too, was crying now. "Yer pa always prayed, 'Yer will be done.' "

"You can pray that way if you want to," said Missie insistently, "but I'm going to tell God exactly what I want. I want Pa. I want him well and strong again. What's wrong with telling God exactly what you want Him to do?"

"Yer pa always says thet we don't be orderin' God — we *ask*."

Missie pulled away, and Marty could feel frustration, even anger, in the slim body. Brushing at her tears, Missie went back to the sandwiches. Her whole person seemed shut away. Marty remained in silent prayer, for Clark and for Missie, as she began to slice beef and place it on the bread.

When the sandwiches and coffee were ready, Missie went to check on Nathan. She held the small boy close and let her tears fall. When she was sure she could speak coherently, she talked to him. "Grandpa got the boys out, Nathan. Grandpa is kind of a hero. He hurt himself saving others. Now he needs to be in bed and have a long rest. You and Josiah might have to be very quiet and especially good for the next few days. You can do that for Grandpa, can't you?"

She felt Nathan's head bobbing a yes up against her.

"We need to pray for Grandpa. God can make him all better again. Will you pray with Mama now, Nathan?"

Nathan agreed and the two of them knelt by his bed.

"God," said Nathan simply, "Grandpa got to be a hero an' is hurt an' needs you to help him. He needs me an' Josiah to be quiet an' not 'sturb him. Help us to not fight or yell. An' help Mama an' Grandma to nurse Grandpa good. Amen."

Missie wished to ask the young boy to pray again. She wanted to say, "Nathan, you didn't ask God to make your grandpa well. You didn't say it, Nathan." Instead she held him for a moment and told him if he'd like to go to the kitchen and share the lunch with the ranch hands, he could. Nathan bounded away, glad to be free of his room.

Missie returned to the kitchen, her heart

heavy and her head spinning. How could God answer their prayers if they didn't pray them? Missie went to pour the coffee with a shaking hand.

When Missie had returned to the kitchen, Marty slipped quietly into Clark's room and knelt by his bed. She took one of his hands in hers and caressed it, careful not to bring further hurt to the already damaged hand. It did look better now that it had been cleaned up. She pressed it to her lips and let her tears wash it again.

"Oh, Clark," she whispered, "I couldn't bear it iffen somethin' should happen to you. Oh, God, I jest couldn't stand it. Please, dear God, make 'im better again. Please leave 'im with me. I need 'im so much." There, she was praying the very way she had warned Missie against. Well, she simply couldn't help it! She needed Clark so much. She loved him more than life itself. She couldn't bear to lose him. She just couldn't! "Oh, please, God — please, please, God," she pled.

She stayed beside his bed, crying and praying, until all her energy and her tears were spent. Clark still did not stir. Would he ever regain consciousness?

At length Marty was aware of a hand on

her shoulder. "Mama," asked Missie, "do you want a cup of coffee?"

Marty shook her head.

"You should, you know. It might be a long night. Wong made supper for the boys. I didn't think anyone else would be hungry."

Marty looked up. "Yer right," she said wearily. "I couldn't eat a bite."

"Coffee, then," said Missie, holding out the cup.

Marty lifted herself to her feet and took it. She was surprised at how stiff she had become and she wondered how long she had been there beside Clark. Missie pushed a chair toward her and she sat down.

"The boys are already in bed," Missie ventured. "Willie still isn't back. Don't know why he —"

"Maybe he went fer a doctor. He said thet yer pa's leg —"

"I'm afraid there's no doctor anywhere around," Missie offered sadly. "He might have heard of someone good at setting breaks, though."

Marty sipped at the coffee and watched Missie's face.

"Didn't Willie say where he was goin'?"

"Just said he would be gone for a while and if we needed anything to call the men. He also said not to let Pa stir around none.

Might hurt his leg."

Marty looked at the motionless Clark. "Looks like we needn't worry none 'bout thet. Wish he *would* stir some. It would make me feel some better iffen I could jest talk to him."

"Willie says that moving might injure his leg even more."

"Maybe it's a blessin' thet he has thet bump on his head. At least he doesn't suffer as much. By the time he comes to again, maybe the pain will be cared fer some."

Marty hadn't thought of the unconsciousness as a blessing, but perhaps it was. She just hoped it wouldn't last too long.

They sat together in silence. Scottie came for a few minutes and asked if there was anything he could do. They assured him they would call if there was any change.

Cookie poked his head around the door, then hobbled in.

"Are you all right?" Missie asked him.

"Whatcha meanin'?" asked Cookie.

"You're lookin' sorta down."

Cookie shook his head. How could he tell her that seeing Clark's injury had reminded him of the injury in his past and the pain that had accompanied it? Clark was truly fortunate right now. He was unaware of pain. But if consciousness returned, would he be able to keep from screaming with the intensity of the agony he would feel? And how would those earth-rending screams affect the rest of the household?

"Guess it bothers me to see a good man hurt" was all Cookie said.

The evening crawled on. The sun disappeared and the stars came out. Soon a silvery moon was shining down on a familiar world. The horses stomped and fought in the corrals, Max barked at some distant coyotes, the crickets chirped, and the night-winged insects beat against the windowpane in an effort to get to the light. Still Clark did not stir, and Willie did not come.

Marty and Missie sat together, talking in low tones and praying in turn. At length Missie stood and moved toward the door.

"I think I'll fix something to drink. Do you want tea or coffee?"

"Tea, I think," responded Marty wearily. She, too, stood and walked about the room. Missie left for the kitchen, and Marty moved to pick up Clark's ragged clothes from the floor. She looked at them. They were dirty and torn and the trousers were minus one leg. Clark's leg? She kept forgetting the broken leg in her anxiety over

Clark's unconsciousness. But she was not overly concerned about the leg. Many people had suffered broken legs. Usually, with a little skill on the part of some attendant, the leg was soon whole and workable again.

Marty pulled back the bedcover and looked at the leg swathed in bulky bandages. *Actually, the men did a rather poor job of it,* she thought. She began to unwind the white material, determined to fix the bandage up a bit. To her surprise there was blood on the cloth. Broken legs did not bleed, unless of course the injury was more extensive. Marty unwound the bandage more hurriedly, and the little cry that escaped her lips was like the sound of a small wounded animal. Clark's leg was not just broken — it was destroyed! Marty felt a sickness sweeping all through her and rushed to the small basin on the stand in the corner. Her whole body shook as she retched. Faint and weak, she grasped the edge of the stand and fought to stand on her feet. At length she regained enough strength and presence of mind to be concerned for the evidence of her sickness before Missie returned. She gathered up the basin and the small pitcher Missie had used for the cold water and headed for the backyard, disposed of the basin's contents and washed it out, and then returned quickly to the room. The cool night air had helped to revive her some, and she hastily attempted to put things back in order. Hurriedly she rewrapped the broken limb, trying to copy the men's original bandaging as closely as she could. Then she chided herself. It was not a time for secrets. She knew Willie had tried to spare her — her and Missie — but the truth needed to be known.

She unwrapped the wound and began to methodically and carefully clean and bind it up, doing the best job possible for her to do. She finished just as Missie returned with the tea.

Marty was glad for the strong, hot tea. She sipped it slowly until she felt some of its strength gradually making its way through her body.

"I took a look at yer pa's leg," she stated as matter-of-factly as she could.

"The broken one?"

"The broken one."

"I hope you didn't move —"

"Yer father did not stir."

A minute of silence followed.

"It's bad, Missie, really bad."

"How bad?"

"A heavy timber or rock must have fallen on it."

"You mean — ?"

"I mean it's crushed. It'll need a real doctor, one with special skills an' tools —"

"Then we'll find one. Willie probably went for one. That's what he did. He went to find a doctor."

"But ya said —"

"What do I know? Just bcause I don't know of a doc doesn't mean there isn't one. Willie hears far more —"

"I hope an' pray he knows of one."

"He will. He will. Just you wait and see. When he gets back here, he'll have —"

The sound of horses came faintly through the window. Missie ran to the door and looked out through the darkness into the yard. No, not horses — a horse. Willie was back, but Willie was alone.

"The doc must be following," Missie called over her shoulder to Marty. "Willie is home now."

Missie ran to meet him. When they returned to the house together, Missie's cheeks bore fresh tears. Marty guessed the meaning.

"Willie had them telegraph every town he knew. Nowhere around do they have a doctor," she confessed. Willie, standing with slumped shoulders and an ashen face, could not speak.

Marty crossed to him. "You've done all thet ya could," she comforted, putting her hand on his shoulder. "Thanks, Willie." She coaxed forth a smile that she did not feel. "We'll jest have to pray even harder," she said.

Three people now sat in silence or moved slowly about the room or spoke in hushed tones. Clark did not stir through the long night.

When dawn came, Willie insisted that Missie get some rest. The children would be needing her. Missie left to lie down for a brief time. Still no change in Clark. The day moved on, from forenoon to noonday, afternoon to evening. Marty left Clark's side only for a few minutes at a time. She was not interested in eating, could not think of sleeping. Her mind was totally focused on her husband lying silently in the bed.

Just as the long day ended and the sun was leaving the sky, Clark stirred and a groan came from his lips. Marty rushed to him. He opened his eyes, seemed to recognize her, and groaned again. He slipped back into unconsciousness, but to Marty it was a blessed sign. Just to see him move and look at her was something to be thankful for. She allowed the tears to stream down her face as she buried it against him.

ELEVEN
STRUGGLES

Clark remained unconscious the entire next day. Marty stayed by his bed, longing to be able to talk with him. Missie came as often as her duties would allow. In the late afternoon Willie returned to the house and insisted that both of the women take a rest. After a bit of an argument, they went, realizing they could not carry on longer without some sleep. Willie had Wong bring him coffee, and he settled himself beside Clark's bedside. He had slept very little himself in the last two days. His eyelids felt heavy and his eyes scratchy. He rubbed a callused hand over his face.

Why did this have to happen? Why? The time they had looked forward to for so long — had dreamed of as a time of joyous reunion — had turned into a nightmare. *Why?* Surely God hadn't brought Clark and Marty way out here to take Clark's life and possibly damage Marty's faith. It was all an enormous puzzle to Willie.

And the boys? He worried about his sons. They had been so excited about meeting their grandparents. Missie had made it a great adventure for them. They had counted the weeks, the days. And then, when they had met their grandparents, they had loved them so quickly, so deeply — and now this tragedy. Poor little Nathan. Not only had his grandfather been taken from him in the last few days but even his grandmother and, thought Willie, his own ma, too. Missie's mind was far too unsettled and troubled by her father's condition to do more than respond to her children's basic needs.

Willie got up and moved to the boys' room. Josiah slept soundly, mostly unconscious of the burden the household was presently bearing, though he probably felt the emotional undercurrents. Nathan was not there; perhaps he was in the kitchen with Wong or visiting Cookie or playing with Max. The poor little fellow. He was trying so hard to be good.

Willie crossed to his own room and looked in on Missie. Though she was sleeping, her face was still pale and drawn. Willie's heart ached for her. He gently smoothed back her long hair and left her.

He looked in on Marty. She, too, slept

soundly. She looked exhausted — as well she might. She had hardly left Clark's side since the accident.

Willie went back to Clark's room. He should check the leg. He pulled back the covers and looked at the neat, fresh bandage. This was not the bandage he had hurriedly wrapped. Someone else had been caring for Clark. Someone else knew of the leg's condition. Willie wiped his hand over his face again. Did the women know? If so, he hated the thought of their suffering this additional burden. At the same time, he felt some of the tension leave him. It would be far better if they did know. It would help prepare them for what likely was ahead.

Willie pulled the light cover up over Clark and sat down heavily in the chair. The house was quiet. Most of its occupants were asleep. Willie, too, dozed occasionally, only to waken to chide himself and determine not to let it happen again.

Josiah must have awakened from his hap and left his bed in search of another family member. Willie, hearing him in the hall, went to get him. He picked up the small boy and held him close, walking back and forth in the hallway and murmuring words of love to him. Josiah cuddled closely against his father, his pudgy hands around his neck and his fingers intertwined in Willie's thick hair. He liked to be held. He liked to be loved. As far as Josiah was concerned, the world had no sorrows.

At length, Willie held the little boy away and looked at him. "Are ya hungry?" he asked.

"Yeah. Where Mama?"

"Mama is restin'. She's very tired."

"Mama sleepin'?"

"Right. Do you want to go see Wong an' have him git ya some milk an' bread?"

"Yeah!" exclaimed Josiah in glee. He always enjoyed a visit with Wong.

Willie carried him to the kitchen. Wong looked up from the table where he and Nathan were cutting doughnuts.

"Aha," said Wong, "small boy is wake now."

"Awake an' hungry, Wong. Ya think ya might have somethin' fer him?"

Wong smiled. He enjoyed the children.

"Yes, yes. Wong find."

Nathan called to Josiah. "Hi, Joey. Ya all done with yer sleep? See what big brother is doin'. Look! I'm helpin' Wong make dough-nuts. We're gonna have 'em fer supper."

"Maybe. Maybe not," said Wong. "Too slow. Maybe tomorrow."

"I'll hurry," said Nathan and began to slap

down the cutter in rapid succession, making weird-shaped doughnuts with chopped-out sides as one cut overlaid another.

"Slow. Slow," called Wong. "We have some for supper. You make slow."

Nathan obliged with more careful cuts. Willie squeezed the boy's shoulder. "I can hardly wait," he said. "Those shore look like good doughnuts." Then he turned to Wong.

"Speakin' of supper, ya wanna jest feed the boys? The women are both havin' a rest, an' I plan to let 'em sleep as long as they can. The boys can play outside fer a while an' then they can eat. I'll jest have a bowl of soup or some stew in the bedroom."

Wong nodded.

Willie returned to the bedroom and took his place beside Clark. There was no change.

The hours crawled by slowly. Cookie came in and stayed with Clark while Willie washed up his sons and readied them for bed. He spent extra time with them, holding them and reading to them, and then he tucked them in and remained in their room until they both dropped off to sleep.

When he returned to the patient, he was surprised to hear Clark groaning. Cookie was bending over him, trying to restrain him from movement.

"He's comin' out of it," said Cookie.

"Don't be surprised if there's some screamin'."

Clark moaned again and fought against his extreme pain, not aware enough to realize where the pain was coming from.

"Don't know how he's gonna stand it when he wakes up a bit more," Cookie muttered, and Willie had the impression Cookie knew firsthand what he was talking about.

Willie feared what Clark's cries might do to the sleeping household.

"Isn't there anythin' — ?"

"Ya watch 'im and try ta hold 'im down," said Cookie. "I'm gonna find Scottie."

Cookie hobbled out, and Scottie soon came noiselessly into the room, breathless from running. Willie watched as he pulled out a small package from his pocket and opened it. Willie did not see the contents of the package, nor did he ask any questions, but Scottie seemed to feel some information was in order.

"A little morphine. Cookie's. He needs it now an' then fer the pain thet still bothers 'im. Makes me keep it so he won't be tempted to take it oftener than he should."

Willie nodded.

Clark was thrashing and moaning, his brow covered with perspiration; his hands tried to clutch at the bedclothes as if to tear away the pain. Scottie leaned over him and spooned the drug into his mouth. It was a while before it took effect, and the men guarded and soothed Clark as they waited for the medicine to work. At last Clark became quieter and eventually fell into a deep sleep. Willie was thankful for the respite. But what would they do when Cookie's small supply of morphine ran out?

It was almost morning before Clark woke again. Willie had been dozing in the chair and was awakened by Clark's moaning. Clark's eyes were open when Willie looked up at him. Though the pain would have been considerable, Clark was rational.

He looked at Willie and, for the first time in three days, seemed aware of his situation.

Willie was relieved to recognize that Clark was alert. At least his mind had not been affected. "How ya doin'?" Willie asked softly, lifting some water to Clark's lips.

Clark sipped very little and then turned his head. A groan escaped him. "Pain" was all he said. "Pain."

"Where does it hurt the most?" persisted Willie. He had to know the extent of the head injury.

"Leg," said Clark.

Willie felt another wave of relief pass through him.

"How's yer head?"

"Hazy . . . little ache . . . all right."

"Good," Willie encouraged.

Clark rolled his head back and forth, the moans escaping from his throat.

"Where's Marty?" he finally asked.

"I made her go sleep fer a while."

This must have satisfied Clark. He lay clenching his jaw to keep the screams from coming. Willie knew he needed more medication and moved the lamp to the window, their prearranged signal.

"How long?" Clark gasped out.

"You've been here fer three nights. It happened the afternoon of the day before."

"The old mine . . . I remember."

It was a good sign. Willie breathed a thankful prayer.

"How're them boys?"

"Haven't heard much since we brought you out," said Willie and let it go at that.

"Did ya get Abe out?"

"His pa did."

"Good."

Clark closed his eyes, obviously trying to fight away the pain and maybe sleep again, but it didn't work. Scottie was soon there, and Clark took the medication without protest. This time he did not sleep as soundly. He dozed off and on. The pain was

189

still with him, but he was able to bear it.

"Didn't give 'im as much," Scottie murmured to Willie. "We gotta ration this here stuff out."

Willie nodded.

The light from the dawn was gently coloring the morning sky. Clark slept, then spoke and slept again. Willie knew Marty was anxious for a word with her husband. Perhaps she had slept enough and needed to be called.

"Scottie, can ya stay a few minutes with 'im? I should wake Mrs. Davis. She'll want to see 'im." Scottie nodded agreement.

Willie woke Marty gently.

"He's awake now. Not too much awake, but he's able to talk some."

Marty threw back the quilt that covered her fully clothed body and scrambled from the bed.

Willie attempted to slow her down. He took her arm.

"He's in awful pain, Ma. It ain't easy to see 'im like thet."

Marty nodded dumbly, but her step did not slow.

When they reached Clark's room, Scottie stepped outside, and Marty threw herself at Clark's bedside and began to weep against him.

He reached out a trembling hand and soothed her hair. He no doubt knew her well enough to let her cry for a while. When her tears were spent, he spoke to her.

"I'm all right. Don't fret yerself." His voice sounded rough but surprisingly strong.

"Shore," she smiled weakly, blinking away tears. "Shore ya are."

"My leg's not too good, though. Ya knowin' thet?"

"I know." The way Marty said it confirmed to Willie that she truly did know. Marty must have been the one who had changed the bandages. Once again, Willie felt a surge of respect for this strong woman.

Clark ran a feeble hand through Marty's tangled hair.

"Yer not lookin' yer best, Mrs. Davis," Clark teased her.

"Thet's funny," said Marty, smiling and wiping away her tears, "ya ain't never looked better."

Willie quietly left them alone.

Scottie was there to portion out small amounts of the morphine as Clark needed it. Clark really could have used far more pain-killer than he was allowed, but once their supply was gone there would be no more.

Clark was able to talk a bit with his visitors. Nathan even was allowed a short visit with his grandpa. He was awed to see his strong grandfather lying pale and still on the bed. But when Clark teased him and rumpled his hair, Nathan looked reassured. Marty and Missie both spent most of their time trying to think of something they could do to ease Clark's pain or restore his body. Missie fussed in the kitchen over special dishes she hoped would encourage her father's appetite. He made a great effort to eat and please her, but even she could tell it was difficult with the dreadful pain always present throughout his whole body.

Word came from town concerning the boys who had been involved in the disaster. Andy seemed to be recovering. His broken ankle had not been crushed, and his parents felt that it would heal in time. They were deeply grateful to Clark for his courageous rescue and sent word that he was in their prayers.

Funeral services were held for Abe. Marty hardly knew how to tell Clark, but she felt he deserved to know. She approached the subject cautiously.

"They say thet Andy's ankle should be

healin'."

"Thet's good," said Clark. "The way thet timber had 'im pinned, I was feared it might be bad broke."

"The other boy — Casey — he's fine. Jest some scrapes an' scratches an' his deep inner pain, I guess. The third boy, Abe, was his younger brother."

"He told me."

"Abe didn't make it, Clark."

"I know." Clark spoke very quietly.

"Ya know?"

"He was already dead when I first found him."

Marty was surprised and, for a moment, angry. "Ya *knew* he was dead when ya risked everythin' to go back on in there an' —"

Clark hushed her with a raised hand. "If it had been our boy, would ya have wanted him out?"

Marty was silent. Yes, if it had been her boy, she would have wanted to hold him one more time.

Marty was deeply relieved at the clarity of Clark's thinking. She was so glad the head injury had not caused permanent damage, but she could not shut from her mind the picture of Clark's leg and the condition it was in. Each time she entered the sickroom, the stench of the injured leg met her with increasing force. The leg was in bad shape. It might even claim Clark's life. Marty fought that thought with her entire being. They needed medicine. They needed a doctor. At times she was tempted to demand that Willie hurry them to the train so they could head for home. In more rational moments Marty knew he'd never survive such a long trip in his weakened condition.

And then Clark began to flush with fever. His eyes took on a glassy look, and his skin was hot and dry. *It's the poison,* admitted Marty to herself, *the poison from the wound.*

Marty could hardly bear this new dilemma. He had been doing well under the circumstances. He had been gaining back a little strength. He had been able to talk. And now this. They had no way to fight this. *Oh, dear God, what can we do?*

At first, they did not talk about Clark's condition, for to talk about it would be to admit it, and also to admit that they were defeated, for they had nothing with which to fight the dreaded infection.

At last Marty knew they could no longer try to pretend that the problem was not there.

"Bring me a pan of hot water," she said to Missie. "An' boil a good sharp pair of yer best scissors. We've gotta do somethin' 'bout yer father's leg."

Then Marty went to find Scottie. Willie and Scottie thought Marty had not noticed the drug ministrations to Clark, so Scottie was caught off guard when Marty walked up to where he was working on the cinch of a saddle and calmly announced, "Scottie, I don't know how much medicine ya still have left, but Clark needs a good-sized dose now. I've got to clean up thet leg the best I can or it's gonna kill 'im. The poison from thet gangrene is goin' all through his system, an' we don't have much time."

Scottie gazed into her face, wonder in his eyes. "Yer a better man than I am," he said, then must have caught his blunder. "Well, anyway, I'm thinkin' I'd not have the stomach to do what yer intendin' to do."

He went for the medicine and gave Clark a large dose. Marty waited until the morphine had taken effect, then gathered together all her limited supplies and every ounce of her courage and went to Clark's room. She threw the window wide open and lit a piece of rag in a tin can to help smoke out the odor, then threw back the light quilt and removed the bandages. It was even worse than she had feared. Never before had Marty faced such a sight and smell. She wanted to faint, to be sick. But she would allow herself neither. She soaked and snipped and cut away dead flesh, but even as she worked she knew she was fighting a losing battle. She finished her difficult task, knowing that what she had done would not be enough.

Gently she covered Clark, all but the damaged leg. She left it exposed to the air, thinking the fresh air might do it some good. Then she cleaned the scissors and knife she had used and put things away in their proper places and went to her own bed.

Down upon her knees, she cried out her anguish to God. She began by telling Him how much Clark meant to her and reminding God of how faithfully Clark had served Him over the years. She told God she had already suffered through the loss of one husband and couldn't possibly bear to lose another. She reminded the Lord of her family at home and of Missie and the grandchildren here. They, too, needed Clark. And then she pleaded and finally demanded that God heal her husband. Hadn't He promised to answer the prayers of His children when they prayed in faith, prayed believing?

Then she returned to Clark. Clark's breathing was just as shallow, his face just as flushed, his brow just as hot as before.

But Marty determined that she would sit right beside him and wait for the Lord's miracle.

Missie came in. At the sight of her father's infected leg, she gave a little cry and, placing her hand over her mouth, ran from the room. Marty's heart ached for her. *What would she ever have done if she'd seen it before I cleaned it up?* thought Marty. Marty was thankful Missie had been spared at least that much.

The drug began to wear off, and Clark tossed and turned in his pain. Marty bathed his hot face and body in an attempt to get the fever down. It had little effect. Clark soon became delirious, and Marty had to call for help to hold him. Willie came and then Cookie, and the two men sent Marty from the room. Marty paced back and forth, back and forth, praying that God's miracle might soon come. Still Clark's screams and groans reached her ears.

Maria came. White-faced and wide-eyed, she stood in the hallway and talked to the tearful Missie. She did not stay long. Clark's agony and the distress of the entire household sent her crying from the home.

The hours crawled by. Marty went into the sickroom occasionally, but Clark's misery was more than she could bear. At last, she went to her room again . . . and again fell beside her bed. This time her prayer was different.

"Oh, God!" she wept from the bottom of her soul. "Ya know best. I can't stand to see 'im suffer so. I love 'im, God. I love 'im so. Iffen ya want to take 'im, then it's all right. I won't be blamin' ya, God. Ya know what's best. I don't want 'im to suffer, God. I leave 'im in yer hands. Yer will be done, whether it's healin' or takin', thet's up to you, God. An', God, whatever yer will, I know thet ya'll give me — an' all of us — the strength we need to bear it."

Marty eventually arose from her knees and went to find Missie. A strange peace filled Marty's being. She still shivered with each scream from Clark. It still pierced her to the quick to know he suffered so, but Marty knew that God was in control and that His divine will would be done.

She found Missie in the boys' room. The boys, however, were not there. Lane had taken them to the barn, where they wouldn't hear their grandfather's agonizing cries.

Missie clutched the small backpack Clark had used to carry her as an infant and that she in turn had used to carry her own sons. She was sobbing out her hurt and anguish.

"Missie," Marty said, taking the girl into

Alameda Free Library

1550 Oak St.

Alameda, CA 94501

510-747-7777

Date: 3/28/2019

Time: 3:21:22 PM

Fines/Fees Owed: $0.00

Total Checked Out: 1

Checked Out

Title: Love's abiding joy
Barcode: 33341007649444
Due Date: 04/18/2019 23:59:59

her arms. "It's gonna be all right. I know it is."

Missie burst into fresh tears. "Oh, I want to believe that. I've been praying and praying for God to make him well."

"He may not," said Marty simply, looking into her daughter's face.

Missie looked at her mother in bewilderment.

"But ya said —"

"I said it will be all right. An' it will. Whatever God decides to do will be the best. He knows us. He knows our needs. He seeks our good. Whatever He wills —"

But Missie pushed her arms away.

"Oh, Missie, Missie," Marty began to sob. "I fought it, too. I fought it with all my bein'. I want yer pa. I want him here with me. But God knows thet. I don't even have to tell 'im. But, little girl, we've got to trust Him. We've gotta let God truly be God."

Missie rose and left the room, still sobbing. Marty heard her close the door to her own room, and she could hear the muffled sobs. There was nothing more that Marty could say. She could only pray.

Marty went to the kitchen to ask Wong for coffee for the men in the sickroom. They had given him the last of the medication, allowing him to sleep once more. Each one in the house felt the lingering question: *What then?*

As Marty carried the pot of coffee and cups to the room, she met Missie in the hall. Her face was still tear-streaked but more serene. "Mama," she said, "I just wanted you to know that it's all right. I've prayed it all through, and I'm . . . I'm willing to . . . to let God be God. He does know best. I knew it all along. It's just easy to forget sometimes when you want your own way so. . . ." She could go no further.

Marty managed a weak smile, and the tears flowed down her cheeks. She leaned over and kissed Missie on the cheek and then straightened to go on to Clark's room. She heard a knock sound on the front door and turned to watch Missie wipe her face with her apron and go answer it.

Missie opened the door, and there stood Maria, her shoulders square and her eyes shining with faith and pride. Just behind her stood Juan.

"Can we come in?" she asked. "My husband . . . is a doctor."

Twelve
Juan

Juan de la Rosa walked purposefully into the sickroom and set his case on the bed. With a quick glance, he took in Clark's pallor and the flushed cheeks. His nose caught the stench of rotting flesh, and he turned to the leg.

He knew even before he looked just what he would find. The crushed limb was badly infected, and the gangrene was not only eating away the flesh of the leg but was also poisoning the man's body.

The leg would have to be removed.

Juan's thoughts went back to another time, one very much like this one. Another man lay before him with a leg in similar condition, and at that time, as well, Juan the doctor had needed to make a life-saving decision. He had decided then, as he was deciding now, that the leg must be sacrificed in order to save the life. All of his training and experience told him so. He had done what he needed to do. And the man had lived.

And then . . . Juan shuddered involuntarily as other memories crowded into his mind. The angry screams, the raging accusations, the shouts of betrayal, and finally the sound of a pistol shot. For a moment, Juan felt he must flee Clark's room — and all those memories. Then the groans of the sick man and the weeping of the women in the hall strengthened him. He straightened himself and looked at the two men in the room.

"I'm going to need lots of boiling water and a strong man to assist me," he said evenly, removing his jacket.

"I wish I could volunteer," said Willie. "I'd like to, but I'm afeared I'd cave in halfway through. I can see to the water, an' I'll find ya a man."

Willie told Marty and Missie about the need for boiling water. Maria, watching nearby, nodded quickly and led the other two women into the kitchen.

At the bunkhouse, Willie found Lane sitting in the doorway watching Nathan and Josiah playing with Max. He went into the bunkhouse, motioned Lane to follow him inside, and shut the door. He looked around at the cowboys in various stages of repose.

"We found us a doc," Willie said. At the

surprise on everyone's faces, he explained, "Well, the Lord found us a doc. It's Juan. Juan has all the trainin' an' has even been in practice fer a few years. I know ya all have questions. So do I, but now ain't the time fer answers. We'll git 'em all in good time. Right now I need a man. I got a job thet won't be easy to do. The doc needs help. He's gonna take off thet there leg. Yer wonderin' why I don't offer, him bein' my father-in-law an' all. Well, I'll tell ya straight out. I'm not sure I could take it. I might fold up on the doc jest when he needs me most. Anyone here think he can do it?"

Willie's eyes scanned the bunkhouse. Some of the cowboys were out on the range taking their shift, but those who were in the room probably wished they were far away, as well, mending fence or herding cattle. Willie had asked a hard thing.

Jake, stretched out on his bunk, had been catching up on some sleep. He'd had the late shift the night before. Smith, the bitter, critical member of the crew, sat in the corner smoking a cigarette and staring at the cards in his hand. Browny was his partner in the game. Clyde, who sat on a stool near the window, shifted the lariat he was working on into the other hand and shot tobacco juice at the bean can on the floor. Lane went white and stared at his hands as though trying to determine whether they would be capable of such a job. The room was heavy with silence. At last, Lane cleared his throat and spoke softly. "I'll do it."

"Ya sure?"

Lane nodded agreement.

"It won't be easy."

Lane recognized that.

"Wish I could help ya . . . I can't promise. Yer sure ya can do it?"

Lane swallowed. "I know *I* can't," he said solemnly. "But I'm . . . I'm trustin' thet *He* can." He motioned upward with his hand.

The religion-hating Smith looked at the silent, shy Lane, a look of grudging respect on his face.

Willie and Lane went to the house, where the doctor was waiting. Willie led the group in prayer; then the men went to Clark's room and the women to the kitchen.

The hands on the clock seemed to drag their way around. The three women had boiled all the water they could find containers for and now sat at a small worktable, untouched coffee cups before them. They had prayed together off and on throughout the whole ordeal, weeping and praising and quoting Bible passages for comfort and encouragement.

"Juan always wanted to be a doctor," Maria began slowly during a pause in the conversation. The other two lifted red-rimmed eyes to her face as they listened to her story. "From the time he was a small boy, he dreamed and planned. At first his father said no. If he wanted to serve, he could be a priest and serve the church. But Juan argued and pleaded. Finally his father said, 'Yes, go ahead, but you will need to pay your own way. My money will not go for foolish dreams.' His father is very wealthy. In his own way, he loves his sons. He wanted both of his boys to stay and ranch with him. Juan went away to the city to school. It was hard. He had to work and he had to study. His father thought he would give up and come home again. But Juan did not. At last he was finished. He was a doctor and was given a good job in a city hospital. His father thought he should come home now. He could be a doctor to the gringos and make good money treating their families, but Juan said no, he must first know more, and then he would come home."

Maria stopped. It obviously was very difficult for her to continue.

"And then one day he was urgently called

home. He must come right away. A man had been hurt. Juan went home and found the injured man. He, too, had crushed his leg. A horse had fallen on him. The leg was too badly broken to fix. It might have been different if he had quickly had a doctor and been taken to a hospital soon. But by the time Juan got there, the leg was like this one. It was infected and stealing away the man's life."

Maria stopped again and took a deep breath.

"He had to take the man's leg. He had to. There was no other choice. Juan did the only thing he could do. The man lived and he again came awake. And then . . . then a dreadful thing happened. He discovered that his leg was gone. He was angry. He screamed at Juan. He wanted to kill him. He said Juan had always been jealous of him and had used his knife to make him less of a man. He screamed and screamed until the father came. He, too, was angry. He sent Juan from the room. And then . . . then there was a pistol shot. Juan ran back to the room. The man had shot himself. Juan's father had not stopped him. The father lay weeping across the body of the dead man. It was his son — Juan's brother."

Missie gasped her horror, and Marty shut

her eyes against the tragedy of it.

"Juan left his father's home," Maria continued after a moment, "and said he would never, never be a doctor again. He hated what he had done to his family. He came to me. I loved him very much. We were planning to be married. Juan said he could not marry me, that he was going far away. That he would never again be a doctor. He threw his bag across the yard and wept as he told me. I said that I loved him. That I still wanted to marry him. That I would go away with him. At last he said I could come. I packed a few things and we went to the village priest, who married us. Juan did not know it, but I packed his medicine bag, as well. It has been hidden these many years.

"We came here and began to ranch. Juan knew ranching. He had been raised on one of the biggest ranches in Mexico. He had ridden and cared for cattle from the time he was a small niño. But still Juan was not happy. He could not forget the past. Nor could he hide the desire to be a doctor."

Maria toyed with the handle of the cup that held the now cold coffee.

"I said that Juan was troubled about coming to church, Missie. About what to teach our little ones. That is right. I did not lie. But Juan is also troubled about other things.

He looks at the boy with the twisted arm and it turns a knife within him. He knows he could have set the arm properly and the boy would not have been crippled. He knows of the boy with the broken ankle in town. He knows that you all suffer here in this house with the good man, Clark. It makes my Juan suffer, too. He has not slept or eaten the last several days. He did not know what to do. He did not know that I had his bag and there was medicine in it."

Maria sighed.

"He will always ask himself, could he have saved the leg if he had come sooner?"

"No," Marty interjected. "He mustn't think that. The leg was crushed. It was a very bad break. I don't think anyone could have saved it. I pretended — but I didn't really believe it. Juan mustn't blame himself. He mustn't. He mustn't blame himself 'bout his brother, either. Juan did what had to be done. He couldn't have done anythin' else."

Maria smiled weakly. "I know that and you know that — and deep down I believe Juan knows that, too. But it still torments him. Only now . . . now I pray he can forget that deep hurt and go on to do what he was meant to do. He was always meant to be a healer, my Juan."

Willie walked into the kitchen, his face pale and his hands looking shaky.

"It's all over," he said, his voice low. "Doc says it went well. Now we jest have to wait an' see."

Marty rose and hurried in to Clark's bedside while Missie and Maria prayed together again.

During the next few days Clark was in and out of consciousness, mostly because of the medication. Dr. de la Rosa, as he was now known, stayed with him, Maria having returned home to their children. Marty found the time following Clark's surgery even more physically and emotionally taxing than her previous vigil, but Juan gave her encouraging reports daily. Clark's pulse was more normal and his color was improving. Juan was hopeful that the infection had been caught in time. Marty dreaded the moment when Clark would be aware of the fact his leg was missing. She worried about how he might respond to the shocking truth.

It happened on the third day following surgery. Clark awoke and seemed to be quite rational. He asked for Marty, who was having her lunch at the time. She went to him, and Dr. de la Rosa left the room.

"I'll be right here in the hall if you need

me," Juan whispered softly as he left.

Marty crossed to Clark's bed.

"Hello there," she said softly. "It's nice to see ya awake. You've been sleepin' a powerful lot lately."

Clark managed a crooked grin. "I reckon," he admitted.

"Ya feelin' some better?"

"I think I'm feelin' lots better than even I know," said Clark.

"Meanin'?"

"Meanin' I've sorta lost track of time an' what's been goin' on. I need a few explanations, Marty. Seems I've been in an' out of a nightmare. Care to fill me in?"

Marty sighed heavily. "It's been a nightmare fer all of us — but I guess fer you, most of all."

Clark waited for her a moment and then prompted, "I think I need to know, Marty."

"Where do ya want to start?"

"How 'bout the beginnin'?"

"Ya remember the mine accident?"

"I remember."

"Ya know thet ya was hit on the head an' were out fer a few days?"

"I do."

"Do ya remember comin' round at all?"

"Yeah. It's sorta hazy. I was in an awful lot of pain. My leg was —"

Clark stopped for a moment, then went on, "My leg's not as bad now."

"We found a doctor. He's been carin' fer ya."

"A doctor! Since I woke up, Juan's been —"

"Juan is a doctor."

"Juan?"

"Right."

"Well, don't thet beat all?" Clark grinned. "How'd thet come 'bout?"

"It's a long story," said Marty. "Juan's been runnin' away from his past. One day I'll tell it all to ya."

"Well, don't thet beat all," Clark said again, shaking his head. "Juan a doctor. Folks hereabouts must be crazy-happy to learn —"

"They's excited 'bout it, all right. Soon's yer well enough to leave without his care, Juan is headin' fer a city to git what he needs to start up a proper-like practice. He's already set the ankle of thet boy in town who was in the mine. He thinks he might even be able to rebreak an' set the arm of the young Newton child. The parents are willin' fer 'im to try."

"Well, I'll be," said Clark and then, after a moment of silent thoughtfulness, he said, "Ya know, this here accident might be worth it if it got a doctor fer this town. Iffen it helped clear up Juan's problems so he could do his proper work again, it jest might be worth the price."

Marty cringed. Clark did not as yet know just how high the price had been.

"So Juan cared for me, huh?" Clark went on.

"He did," answered Marty, "right when we had 'bout given up."

"I was thet bad?"

"Thet bad."

"He had the proper medicine?"

"Enough fer it to do the job. Heard him fussin' thet he didn't have a certain somethin' else, but I guess what he *did* have worked."

"An' he fixed my leg."

"He saved yer life," said Marty.

"He fixed my leg an' saved my life."

Marty did not answer. She bit her lip and then realized Clark was waiting for her to go on.

"Clark," she said slowly, "yer leg was bad broke. It wasn't just a break, Clark. It was crushed. Then it got even worse. It got all infected with gangrene. The gangrene's poison nearly killed ya. It would have, too, if it hadn't been fer Dr. de la Rosa."

Clark's face had gone white as Marty said

the words *gangrene* and *poison.*

"An' yer sayin' — ?" His voice was husky with emotion.

"I'm sayin' thet Dr. de la Rosa fixed yer leg as best he could . . . in the only *way* he could. . . . He took it off, Clark. He took it off 'fore it killed ya."

Clark turned away his face. Marty saw a deep shiver vibrate all through him. She threw her arms around him and held him close. She waited for a moment until the reality of it had time to penetrate.

"Clark," she said, her tears falling freely, "I know thet isn't what ya wanted to hear. I know ya didn't want to lose a leg. I didn't want it, either, Clark. With my whole bein', I fought it. But it was yer leg or *you.* For a while, it looked as if it would be both. Oh, Clark, I'm jest so thankful to God thet He sent a doctor along in time to spare ya. I . . . I . . . I don't know how I'd ever make it without you, Clark. God spared ya, an' I'm so glad. So glad. We'll git by without the leg . . . I promise."

Clark smoothed her hair and held her close. His trembling eventually stopped. He could even speak. "Yer right. It'll be all right. Guess it jest takes some gettin' used to."

And then Marty just let herself go and

cried out all of her pent-up worries and frustrations. "Oh, Clark," she sobbed. "I'm sorry. So sorry it had to happen to you like this. If I coulda jest taken yer place. . . . I know how important it is to a man to be whole — to be able to feed an' care fer his family. I could have done my carin' from a chair. It wouldn't have mattered near as much to me. Oh, Clark! I'm so sorry."

"Hush now, hush," said Clark. "Yer actin' like one a' those hysterical woman. This don't change things. I can still care fer my family. One leg ain't gonna make a lot of difference. Hush, now. Iffen the Lord hadn'ta figured I could do without my leg, He wouldn't've 'llowed this, now would He?"

At length, Clark got Marty comforted and in control. He pushed her gently away from him. "An' now," he said, "if ya don't mind, I'm feelin' in need of some rest. I'll talk to ya in the mornin'. Now you send thet there doc back in here, will ya?"

Marty left the room and sent in Juan. Juan entered the room, his pulse racing as he remembered the other incident when his brother had discovered his missing limb. He didn't blame any man for taking the news hard. He stood silently, looking at the big man lying still on the bed. Clark was the first to speak.

"I hear I owe ya my life."

Juan said nothing. Perhaps Clark did not yet know about his leg.

But Clark went on. "It must be a powerful hard decision fer a man to make — even a man trained in medicine — to take a man's limb an' spare the man's life, or let him die with both legs on. I'm glad I've never had to do the choosin'. I want to tell ya 'thank you' for bein' brave enough to make the choice fer me when I wasn't able to make it fer myself. I would have chosen to live, Juan — even without the leg — I would have chosen to live. Life is good — an' life is in the hands of almighty God. Now, I'm not sayin' I fancy learnin' to live without a leg. I'm not pretendin' to be some hero thet it won't bother none. But I am sayin' 'thank you' fer givin' me thet chance. With God's help, I'll make it. If He 'llowed it, then He must have a plan to git me through it, too. Fer He plans only fer my good."

Juan stood watching Clark — no angry cries, no cursing, no incriminations coming from the man. Clark knew of his handicap — he knew of his great loss — but he had accepted it and even thanked the doctor for giving him a chance to live. There was a difference here. A distinct difference between the way this man accepted his handicap and the way his own brother had. What made the difference? Juan determined to do some thinking on it when he could get off by himself and take the time. One thing he already knew — where his brother had cursed God, this man thanked God. Perhaps . . . perhaps it had something to do with that.

Clark interrupted his thoughts. "An' now, Doctor, I don't be pretendin' thet this here situation hasn't shook me up a bit. It's gonna take some gittin' used to the idea. I don't much feel up to thinkin' 'bout it at the moment. Ya happen to have somethin' to help a man git a little sleep instead? It might all be easier to handle come mornin'."

Dr. de la Rosa moved to prepare some medication.

Clark did not go to sleep immediately. He spent time thinking, even though he wished he could shove the whole problem off to the side and pretend it did not exist. He also did some praying — deep soul-searching conversation with the Almighty, asking for God's help in the hours, days, and weeks ahead of adjustment and growing. He even did some weeping — heartrending sobs that shook his large frame. When it was all over, he wiped the tears from his gaunt cheeks, set his chin, and reached for the unseen hand of God. It was a very long time before he discussed his feelings concerning his handicap again.

Thirteen
Adjustments

Marty thought Clark's recovery was slow indeed, but to Dr. de la Rosa, it was a daily miracle. Clark was doing much better than the doctor had dared to hope. When one considered what the man had been through, his convalescence was truly amazing, Doc often told her.

Willie had kept the family in the East informed throughout the whole ordeal by the means of telegrams. A great measure of relief accompanied the cable assuring them that Clark was well on the way to recovery. He stated that, at the present, he was still unable to give them a date for Clark's return home. The answer soon came by telegram: "PA DON'T HURRY STOP EVERYTHING FINE HERE STOP LETTER FOLLOWING." Marty anxiously awaited the arrival of the letter.

As she sat one morning mending one of Nathan's small shirts, Marty was surprised to realize it was well past the time they had planned to return to their farm. How different the trip had turned out from what they had expected! It dawned on Marty that Clare's wedding was only days away. She and Clark would not — could not — possibly make it back in time. Deep disappointment flooded through her. How could she miss her son's wedding? But neither would she want the young couple to postpone it on their account. Then Marty thought of Luke's plans to go off to college. She should be home right now preparing his clothes and getting him ready. How she hated to miss that, too! A few tears slipped down her cheeks, and Marty wiped them away quickly before they could be observed. *But Luke is so young,* her heart cried. It was hard enough to let him go, but without her there to . . . She stopped herself. She'd be crying in earnest if she didn't get her imagination under control.

Marty laid aside the shirt and went to check on Clark. Missie was already there. In fact, it was not often that Missie was *not* with her father. She made up games to play with him, read to him, fluffed his pillows, sponged his face and hands, talked to him about her garden and children, discussed his meals, and told him of happenings in the district. Yes, Missie was often with her father. It was touching to see so much love between father and daughter. Marty smiled at the two of them.

"Do you know what he's saying?" said Missie in exasperation. "He's saying that he's going to get up."

Marty smiled again. "I think thet's a great idea."

"Great?" Missie exclaimed, shocked. "He's not ready for that yet! Juan said —"

"Juan said he should choose his own pace. Iffen yer father thinks he is —"

Clark stopped the two of them. "Hold it, hold it," he said, raising his hands in his customary way. "No use ya all gittin' into it. I will obey my doctor. I'll not git up till I'm good 'n' ready to git up. Iffen ya don't think the time is right, Missie, I'll wait."

Missie looked relieved and Marty slightly bewildered.

"I'll wait until right after lunch," Clark announced.

Missie sputtered, "Big wait — especially since it's now eleven-thirty."

All three began to laugh.

After lunch Clark sat on the edge of the bed for a while. Later, with Marty on one side and Wong on the other, he moved to the porch to sit in a rocking chair. The day was hot, but Marty could tell the sun's rays felt good to this man who had been shut away in the house far too long. He took great breaths of the fresh air and sniffed deeply of the earth and growing things.

Nathan came to play by him, showing him all the tricks Max could do. Being a family dog rather than a show dog, Max had very few of them, so Nathan put him through the same ones over and over while Clark laughed appreciatively as though enjoying each trick.

Marty tried to keep herself from hovering over him, but she watched carefully for any signs he might be overdoing it.

Just then Scottie returned from town with the promised letter from the family back home.

Excitedly, Marty read it aloud.

"Dear Ma and Pa,
   "We are so glad to hear that Pa is finally feeling better. We can't say how sorry we are for the accident that took Pa's leg, but we are so glad that he was spared. We have all been praying daily, I guess almost hourly, for you both.
   "We don't want you to worry a bit about things here at home. Clare has decided to go ahead with his wedding.

They had talked of waiting until you were back home again, but they thought that might pressure you into traveling before you are really ready. We want to be good and sure you are strong enough for the trip before you attempt it, Pa. So, for our sake, please don't come home until you are really well.

"Arnie is taking good care of the stock. That's been his job since you left, Pa. Of course he helps Clare in the field, too, but the stock is in his special care. He has not been seeing Hester lately. Her brothers just made it too miserable, and she says she doesn't want to marry anyone that her brothers can't drink with.

"There's a new girl in town, though. She is the new preacher's daughter, and Arnie has gotten pretty friendly with her. You would really like her, Ma. She's a very thoughtful person, and Arnie is beginning to think she's kind of cute.

"Luke's not going to college this fall. He's been spending a bit of time with Dr. Watkins lately. Dr. Watkins says he's still plenty young and another year of waiting won't hurt him any. Dr. Watkins is giving Luke the use of some of his medical books to read. He is taking Luke with him on his Saturday calls, too, so Luke says he is learning more than he ever would in the first year of medical school. Dr. Watkins really seems to be enjoying Luke. He treats him as though he were his son. Guess Dr. Watkins maybe misses not having a family of his own. Anyway, Luke seems really happy with this arrangement.

"Everything is going well here. The canning is almost all done, Ma. The garden has done real good and the apples are coming on well. Ma Graham came over and helped me for one day. She sends her love. Everyone at church is remembering you in prayer.

"Nandry and Clae both say they will write now that we know a little better what to say. I will admit we were really scared for a while. God bless you both. We miss you to be sure, but we are doing fine on our own.

"In love,
Ellie and the boys"

The letter both relieved and saddened Marty. She missed them all so much, but it was good to hear they were all right and managing well in spite of the extended absence. She was glad Clare was going

223

ahead with the wedding, and she was also glad Arnie had a nice girl for a friend. Marty was relieved to hear that her Luke would not be going off to college without his mother there to see him off. She quietly thanked God for working out these things and for allowing Dr. Watkins to shepherd the boy.

Clark turned from the letter with relief on his face. Marty had been unaware that, in spite of his ordeal, he also was concerned for the family at home.

"Well," he said, "seems as though they be makin' do jest fine without us. I'm proud of the young'uns you've raised, Mrs. Davis." He reached over from his chair for her hand.

Marty beamed. "An' so am I. 'Course you didn't have much of a hand in it at all."

"Maybe we can jest sort of take our time recuperatin' after all," sighed Clark. His grin was a little wobbly. "I think I'll jest get on back to my bed and catch me a nap."

Marty looked at him quickly and saw he was rather pale. Maybe Missie *had* been right . . . maybe Clark was pushing things too quickly. She and Wong got him settled back in his bed.

But Clark was content to take one day at a time. He attempted only what he thought he could manage. Very gradually, his strength was returning.

The two couples from town whose boys had been involved in the mine accident came out to the LaHaye ranch for a visit. The two mothers, still unable to talk of the incident without weeping, thanked Clark over and over for going in after their sons. Mrs. Croft, whose Abe had been lost in the mishap, wiped away tears as she talked about how difficult the adjustment to life without Abe had been for his brother Casey and his parents. But she was so thankful they had been able to see Abe again and that his body had not been buried deep in the mine. They also were appreciative to Willie for taking charge of arrangements concerning the blasting of the mine opening so there would be no further danger to other children.

Though it was difficult for them to truly express what they were feeling, they did try to make Clark understand how sorry they were that he had lost his leg. Clark assured them that in every circumstance of his life — whether good or bad — he believed with all of his heart that God knew his situation and was more than able to help him through it. He told them he was aware that there would be adjustments and some of them would be difficult. But, when it came down to it, though *he* was human, *God* was sovereign. The visitors looked a trifle uneasy at Clark's forthrightness about his faith, and Marty, watching them with understanding, supposed it was as new to them as it had been to her when she had first joined Clark's household so many years before. Clark's face and voice held such confidence that in spite of their doubts, those in the room could not but be sure he believed every word.

Finally Mrs. Croft must have dared to speak some of what she was feeling. "It was hard fer me not to have a preacher man here fer my son's buryin'. Oh, I know I ain't rightly what you'd call a church person, but I believe in the Almighty. Can't say I'm on speakin' terms with 'im exactly . . . but . . . well, sometimes . . . 'specially in hard times like we jest been through . . . sometimes I jest wish I knew a little more 'bout 'im. . . ."

Willie spoke up then. "We have meetin's here together each Sunday. I know it ain't like being in a church, but we do read from the Word together an' sing a hymn or two. Ya all sure would be welcome to join us. Anyone is welcome anytime."

"Where ya meetin'?"

"Right here — in our home."

The woman's face expressed a new interest.

"What time ya meet?"

"Every Sunday at two o'clock."

"I dunno," interjected her husband. "It's a long way from town. By the time we got back home again, it'd be 'most dark."

The woman, disappointed, looked down at her lap and her clasped hands.

Clark suggested, "Maybe the service could be moved up a bit earlier and not 'llowed to go fer too long."

The woman raised her head again, her eyes hopeful.

"Well," said the man, probably sensing how much it meant to her, "we might give it a try fer a Sunday at the two-o'clock time an' see how it goes."

The slight smile flickering across the woman's face said it all.

Andy's parents had taken no part in the exchange about church. Willie turned to them. "We'd be most happy to have ya join us, too."

The man shook his head and shuffled his feet in an embarrassed fashion. What he mumbled was, "Don't think we be needin' thet. Our boy's jest fine now. Doc set his ankle and it's 'most as good as new."

Marty could tell that both Clark and

Willie were biting their tongues to keep from jumping in with an answer.

Finally Clark said, "We spend a bit of time in our service thanking the Lord, as well. Perhaps you an' yer wife would like an opportunity to thank God thet He 'llowed yer boy to git out safely. Ya'd be welcome to join us anytime — fer any reason."

The man nodded silently.

Missie served them coffee and cake, and they went on their way. As she went out the door, Mrs. Croft whispered that she was already counting the days until Sunday.

Maria and Juan came often. Juan, like a new man, had been to the city to make arrangements for setting up a proper office for the practice of medicine. He had stocked a supply cupboard with the medicines and equipment he would need. The townsfolk had coaxed him to move into a building they would provide, but Juan wished to remain on his ranch. He did agree to be at a town office for two days of the week; the rest of the time he would work out of his own home. Glad that he had built a large house, he immediately converted one wing into an office and small examining room. He worried some, realizing that he had none of the conveniences of the city hospitals, but he could send some more serious cases out by train or stagecoach.

One night as they talked together, Clark noticed that the usually buoyant Juan was quiet. Maria tried to keep the conversation going, but it was easy to sense that something was troubling Juan. After asking about his new practice, the neighborhood, the ranch, and the children, and still getting very little response from Juan, the group grew quiet.

Clark eventually turned once more to Juan. "I'm a wonderin', Doc, if I might see ya in the privacy of my room fer a few minutes," asked Clark. Juan offered his arm and Clark managed the distance with short, awkward hops.

Clark sat on his bed and caught his breath. He needed some kind of a crutch. He must get busy fashioning one. Hopping was far too difficult and drained him of what little strength he had.

"Something troubling . . . ?" began Juan, concerned.

"Yah," said Clark easily, "I'm thinkin' there is."

The doctor automatically reached for the offending limb and began to unpin the pant leg, but Clark stopped him. "Leg's jest fine, Doc."

Juan was puzzled.

"Something else is bringing you pain?"

"Well, ya might say thet."

"And where is it hurting?"

"Well, I don't rightly know. Thet's what *I* was gonna ask."

Juan's puzzled frown deepened.

"Well," said Clark, watching Juan closely, "I kinda got the feelin' somethin' was hurtin' the doctor and he wasn't feelin' free to say anythin'."

Juan looked startled and moved away to the window, where he stood looking out on the soft night.

"It shows that much?"

"It shows."

"I am indeed sorry. I did not mean to bring my feelings to this home, to bring sadness to those I care for."

"Anythin' thet ya care to talk about . . . or thet I could do?" asked Clark.

Juan stood in silence for several minutes and finally turned with a deep sigh and troubled eyes.

"I think that you have heard my story — at least in part. You know that I became a doctor against my father's wishes. You know, too, that I was responsible for my own brother's death —"

But Clark's hand stopped him. "No," he

said emphatically, "thet's not the way I heard the story. Yer brother had gangrene in a bad leg; you amputated, as you had to. Yer brother chose to take his own life."

Juan waved that aside. "My father does not see it that way. He told me to leave that night and forbade me to return to his home again."

"I'm sorry," said Clark. "It must be very hard for you."

"It is. It is very hard. Now that I am again going to practice medicine, I wish with all of my heart that I could do so with my father's blessing." Juan hesitated, then continued. "That sounds very foolish to you, I'm sure, but —"

"Not at all. I think I'd feel the same way."

"You would?"

"To be sure I would."

There was silence. Clark broke it. "What of yer mother? Is she still livin'?"

"I don't know. Perhaps that's what bothers me most. My mother never dared to say so, but I think she was proud that I had chosen to be a doctor. When my father sent me away, my mother, for the first time in her life, dared to protest. She fell on her knees before him and pleaded that he reconsider. In the name of Mary and all the saints, she asked him to allow me to stay.

'Must I lose both my sons on the same night?' she cried. I can see her yet, and the vision haunts me. If only I knew that my mother was all right."

"Why don't ya jest go on down an' find out?"

"Return home?"

"Sure."

"But my father has not asked me to come."

Clark shrugged his shoulders.

The minutes dragged by as Juan struggled with the thought. Then Clark asked softly, "Are ya afraid?"

"Of my own father?" Juan's shock showed the insult of such a question.

"Well, I don't know the man. Have no idea what he might do."

"My father would never harm me, if that's what you're thinking."

"I'm thinkin' nothin'," responded Clark simply. "You were doin' the thinkin'."

Juan nodded his head in reluctant agreement.

"So," said Clark, "since ya have nothin' to fear, why is it a problem to go back?"

"I have not been asked," said Juan with a great deal of dignity. "To go back so would be like a stray puppy crawling home for forgiveness and acceptance. Even my father would scorn such —"

"Ya mean it's a matter of pride?" Clark asked quietly.

Juan's head jerked up, his black eyes flashing fire.

"I understand," Clark nodded gravely. "A man does have his pride."

There was silence again. Juan began to pace the room. The air around them seemed to be heavy with unspoken ideas. Clark again dared to break the silence.

" 'Course a man can, with God's help, swaller his pride an' do what he knows he should. If yer mother is livin', I'm sure she is hurtin', too. She has no idea if you're alive or dead. An' if yer father is still livin' an' has maybe changed his feelin's some, how would he ever find ya to let ya know?"

Still Juan struggled with the issue.

"You do not know —" he began.

"No," agreed Clark, "I do not know. I admit to thet. But God does, an' I don't think *you're* admittin' to thet. Shore thing, I wasn't raised like you was, but things have been a bit tough fer me at times, too. Life can be pretty quick to take a swipe at a man. Sometimes we can't duck the blows. We jest gotta take 'em head-on. They smart a bit, to be sure. But . . ." Clark allowed his gaze to rest on his stub of a leg. "He knows all thet.

He not only knows, but He cares. He doesn't ask from us thet we *understand* or even *like* what we face, but jest thet we face it like a man, an' do what we know to be right, even though it goes against us at times."

"And the right thing for me as you see it?"

"I can't tell ya thet. I know thet if yer troubled 'bout things as they are now, maybe ya should do somethin' to try to straighten 'em out. I know mothers can hurt somethin' awful, not knowing 'bout their sons. I know fathers can make mistakes thet they suffer fer, an' sometimes it's most difficult to be man enough to say they was wrong. Thet's all I know. Yes . . . I know another thing, as well. I know God can help us do the right thing — even though it seems impossible. But only you can decide what is the right thing fer you."

Juan weighed the words of the older man. At length he turned to him and extended his hand.

"I am not making any promises, except that I will think about what you have said. It is a very hard thing."

Clark took the hand and shook it firmly. "I'll be prayin' you make the right decision," he said.

They returned to the others. There were questions in many eyes, but none were asked. Maria and Juan soon declared that they must be on their way home.

Cookie came to visit Clark whenever his work would allow him a break. He usually waited until he saw Clark out on the veranda getting some fresh air or early-morning sun, and then he would hobble over to ease himself to a step or a nearby chair. He seemed to feel he and Clark had much in common. One day he even dared to talk about it.

"Leg bother ya much?"

"Not bad now. Gives me a bit of a jar if I happen to bump it."

"Any trouble with 'phantom pain'?"

"Some."

"Must be a peculiar feelin'. Somethin' hurtin' thet ain't even there."

"Yah, bothers me some, all right. Itches somethin' awful at times, an' ya ain't got nothin' to scratch." Clark chuckled ruefully.

"Well, at least I don't have them prob-lems," said Cookie.

"Yer leg still bother ya a good deal?" asked Clark.

"Sometimes." There was a moment of silence while Cookie thought of the pain.

"Not as bad lately, though. Was a time I near went wild with it."

Clark nodded his head in understanding. "How many years now?" he asked.

"I try to fergit. Guess it must be 'bout five already. No, six. Lotsa folks said as how I'da been better off to have it removed like you done."

"Well," Clark reminded him, "I wasn't able to do my own choosin'. Don't know's I'da really picked this way to do it, iffen I had."

"Yer leg was bad broke, Clark," Cookie assured him evenly. "I knew as soon as I seed it thet only a miracle could save it, an' seems to me we been a little short on miracles in my lifetime."

Clark smiled. "Well," he said firmly, "I ain't seen an overabundance of miracles myself, but I shore ain't doubtin' them none." Watching Cookie's expectant face carefully, Clark went on, "Guess one of the biggest miracles I know of is when God takes a no-good sinner and makes a saint fittin' fer heaven outta 'im. Now, thet's a real miracle, to my thinkin'. With some trainin' an' the right tools an' medicine, even an earthly fella like the doc can put a badly messed-up body together again. But only God, through His love an' grace, can take a

236

crushed and broken soul and restore it again. Yes sir, *thet's* a miracle."

Cookie scuffed the dust with the toe of his boot.

"Take me now . . ." Clark said confidingly, "ya know what happened with me? When I first woke up to the fact thet I had only one leg, a part of me died inside. I started tellin' myself all kinds of stories 'bout bein' only half a man, an' how sad it was to be a cripple, an' how sorry I could be fer myself, an' even how God had let me down. Fer a minute, I almost had me convinced thet I had good reason to jest turn over to the wall and have a real good feelin'-sorry-fer-myself time. My body was broken . . . was bruised and hurtin' . . . an' my soul wanted to sympathize with it, see? My soul wanted to curl up an' hurt an' suffer an' become bitter an' ugly. Now, God didn't choose to do a miracle on this here leg." Clark tapped the stump lightly. "But He did a bigger an' more important miracle. He worked over the inner me — the soul of me. Thet's where I needed the miracle the most, so thet's where He applied His amazin' power. In here" — Clark pointed to his broad chest — "I don't hurt anymore."

Cookie's eyes hinted ever so slightly of unshed tears, and Clark wondered how many years Cookie had been in pain both inwardly and outwardly. He reached out a hand and gently squeezed the cowpoke's shoulder.

"We needn't fear." His voice was almost a whisper. "He's still doin' miracles."

FOURTEEN
GROWING

In the fall Willie returned to the range and the business of ranching. Cattle needed to be rounded up and a few stray dogies branded. The steers for market required cutting and sorting from the herd and then would be driven to the train station for shipping. Sagging and broken fences were repaired and pastures checked out before the coming winter, including the all-important water holes for the cattle. And of course the dreaded rustlers mandated constant vigilance. The warm fall days were busy from dawn till dark at the LaHaye spread.

Missie still tried to spend most of her time with her father. Occasionally her own responsibilities suffered because of the attention she was showering on Clark — reading to him, though Marty thought that was one of the things he could do well on his own, making favorite dishes for him, and talking about this and that so his confinement would not seem too burdensome. But Missie's two little boys did not seem to fare too badly, because they also were usually hovering closely around their grandfather.

Soon, though, Marty was noticing that Willie, who came back at night exhausted from his day full of hard work and the pressures of running the spread, was getting little consideration from his wife. Missie was so busy fussing over Clark that she scarcely had time to notice. Marty hoped she was exaggerating things and tried to tuck her anxiety into the back of her mind. She attempted to take care of Clark so fully that Missie would not feel this was her duty, but this did not ease the situation. Missie still hovered close by.

Marty then turned some of her own attention toward Willie, hoping to at least make him aware that he was still loved and appreciated. She of course was fully aware that Willie needed the attention of his wife — not his mother-in-law. Even the boys did not run to meet Willie with the same exuberance at the end of the day, for they had spent the day with a grandfather who carved them tops and fashioned whistles and answered their every question with serious attention.

In spite of her determination to put the matter aside, Marty daily felt her concern grow. To her surprise, Clark, who was normally so sensitive to the feelings of others and aware of situations, did not seem to notice it. Perhaps he was just too close to it.

Marty put her worries into fervent prayers for the Lord to intervene as He saw fit.

Henry came to see Clark. He obviously had something on his mind. After a simple greeting, he came directly to the point.

"Been doin' a great deal of thinkin' lately," Henry said. "We really need us a church."

Clark nodded his head in agreement and looked up from the crude crutch he was carving, having determined it was time he did something to aid in walking. "Good idea."

"Seems like now would be as good a time as any to be plannin' fer it," Henry went on. "I know thet now ain't a good time at all fer ranchers. Real busy time of the year, but things will be slowin' down again 'fore too long. But we shouldn't wait fer things to slow down 'fore we git started. Thet's sorta like puttin' God last. Been thinkin' thet we really are in need of some preachin'. We read the Bible together, an' thet's good, but some of these folks need someone to explain what it's meanin'. Take thet there new family thet's been comin' — the Crofts — they need someone to tell them what the Word means, to show them how to accept the truth fer themselves."

"I was thinkin' thet when ya said 'church' ya was meanin' a buildin'," Clark noted.

"Well, I was, an' I wasn't," answered Henry. "Shore, we need a buildin', an' I think we could work on thet real soon, too. But I was also thinkin' of people an' of those who need to know the truth. I think it's time to give 'em more'n we been doin'."

"Sounds good to me," responded Clark. "Ya got some plans fer this?"

"Yah," said Henry, "been thinkin' on you."

"Me?" Clark couldn't keep the surprise from his voice.

"Shore. You." Henry did not waver.

"But I don't have any Bible trainin'."

"Ya been studyin' it fer years, haven't ya?"

"Yah, but —"

"An' you've heard lots of preachin'?"

"Shore nuff."

"An ya believe the Holy Spirit can teach the truth?"

" 'Course I do."

Henry grinned. "An' ya ain't overly busy these days, are ya?"

Clark couldn't help but chuckle. "No," he

said, "I ain't over busy. Been makin' a few tops an' whistles, an' tyin' a few knots, an' eatin', an' complainin', an' makin' folks run around waitin' on me. Come to think on it," he said, scratching his head with the blunt end of his knife, "seems I been powerful busy after all."

They laughed together.

"Well?" spoke Henry, turning serious.

"Well," responded Clark, "I need to do some thinkin' an' prayin' 'bout thet one."

"You do thet," encouraged Henry and straightened up. He looked quite confident about where Clark's thinking and praying would lead him.

"Gotta git," said Henry. "The fellas will be wonderin' where their boss has disappeared to. See ya come Sunday." And he swung up into the saddle and left the yard at a canter.

Clark continued the work on his crutch, but his thoughts were far away from the task at hand. He paused occasionally to wipe away a tear or two. Maybe God was indeed turning this whole tragic accident into something far beyond what any of them could have imagined.

The group that gathered on Sunday in the large living room of the LaHaye household had again increased. With the Crofts were two other women from town and their children. One was the mother of Andy, the boy Clark had rescued from the mine. The other woman, young and sad looking, had just buried an infant son.

Four of the LaHaye cowboys sauntered in and took inconspicuous seats toward the back of the room, clearing their throats and fingering their wide-brimmed hats self-consciously as they waited for the singing to begin. The simple service was just starting when Cookie hobbled in with a reluctant-looking Wong in tow. Cookie had privately told the family he was going to get Wong to come by telling him this would be a good opportunity to add some new English words to his vocabulary.

Henry led the singing with his guitar, and Willie read the Scripture. After a time for prayer and another song, Willie allowed anyone from the congregation to share a Scripture or a thought. Henry rose to his feet. Clearing his throat, he began slowly with great seriousness.

"Ya all know as how we been feelin' the need to git together like this Sunday by Sunday to hear the Word an' pray. Maybe ya all 'preciate it as much as I do, but ya still feel somethin' is missin'. Like we need to learn more 'bout the Bible. Thet's why churches have preachers — to explain the meanin' of God's Word. Well, we ain't had us a preacher. 'Course we do have the Holy Spirit as our teacher, an' I thank God fer thet.

"This here summer Missie an' Willie had the blessin' of Mr. and Mrs. Davis comin' fer a visit. It was jest to be a short one — a couple a' weeks. We all know the tragic circumstances thet bring 'em to still be here. I say 'tragic' 'cause thet's the way it seems to all of us. But I been thinkin'. Maybe God can bring good outta even this tragedy. The Word says thet all things can work together fer our good if we love God. Lately I've been thinkin' 'bout some good thet might come from this. I spoke to Mr. Davis 'bout it, an' he promised to pray on it. I've asked Mr. Davis if he won't be our preacher an' explain the Word to us Sunday by Sunday. Now, he ain't a preacher, really. He's a farmer. But he knows the Word of God, an' he's heard lotsa preachin', an' I think he'd have lotsa good Bible teachin' to share with us."

Faces began to turn toward Clark, and it was apparent many people were waiting expectantly to see how he would answer. Clark looked around him at the strange little congregation. Missie and Willie, along with

245

Henry and Melinda, had grown even more in their faith since coming west. Rough cowhands sat before him, probably knowing very little about the Bible but seeming to be open to learning more. The sad young woman from town was obviously longing for some kind of comfort. The Crofts also needed healing for their recent bereavement. The family with the son whose arm still needed to be straightened sat with the group, along with Andy beside his mother. The de la Rosas had joined them that day, and the pain and the questions still lingered in Juan's eyes. Clark's heart went out to them all. He felt a strange stirring within, and he knew that, with God's help, he must feed this flock. He stood up, his crutch held firmly in hand for support, and looked around at the faces before him.

"It honors me to be asked to open God's Word with ya here. With God's help, I will try to give to ya the meanin' of the Scripture read each Sunday. We can learn together."

He sat down, and enthusiastic nods and smiles swept around the room. Marty was so proud and happy she could have put her head against Clark's shoulder and wept tears of joy.

Henry stood again, his face beaming. "We got us a preacher!" he exulted. "Now, what we gonna do 'bout a church? We're gettin' to be too big a crowd to fit here anymore."

There were enthusiastic and spontaneous responses to the question. Many voices began to call that they would build their own church, and some made suggestions about where it should be located. Henry finally got things quieted enough to speak again.

"I've been thinkin'," he said, "thet since there's not a church in town yet, an' this is a powerful distance fer some to travel, we oughta try to even things up a bit an' put the church 'bout halfway fer everyone."

"I'm 'bout halfway!" exclaimed Mr. Newton, jumping to his feet. "I shore would be right proud to be givin' some of my land fer a church."

Others nodded, their faces full of enthusiasm and anticipation. It was agreed that the church building could be located on the Newton ranch. "We'll need us timber an' materials an' a buildin' plan," said Henry. "Lots of things to be decided."

"Then let's git us a committee," someone called.

Eventually the group concluded that Willie, Henry, and Mr. Newton would be the building committee. The rest of the congregation would wait for orders and do their bidding. Excitement ran so high that tongues could not slow down even when Missie served coffee and cookies. They were going to have their own church! A dream come true.

Marty wrote another long letter to send east. They would not be returning home to the farm and the rest of their family until the next spring. Though Clark was daily gaining strength and would now be able to tolerate the train trip, he was going to stay and help establish the new church, giving the people lessons from the Scriptures and encouraging them in their building project.

Marty was pleased to see the enthusiasm with which Clark greeted each new day. He spent hours poring over his already-well-used Bible, and as his heart discovered new truths, his lips shared them with others. He often could not wait for Sundays but spoke excitedly with anyone who was within listening distance.

Clark also was busy with other matters, thinking about little inventions that would help him in overcoming his handicap. Daily his independence was growing. He scarcely needed aid any longer. He even adapted a saddle so he could again ride horseback with the men or with Nathan. He moved about the ranch on his own, carrying buckets or saddles in the hand that wasn't occupied with the crutch. He went out to the garden and helped to dig the last of Missie's vegetables. He went with Nathan to gather eggs and prepared fryers for Sunday dinner. Marty marveled and rejoiced as she watched him move about with confidence and assurance.

Marty knew that Missie, too, was glad to see her father up and around again. But she still could not seem to keep from fussing overly much. Marty realized it was Missie's admiration for her father that was motivating her — trying to make him comfortable whenever she came near him, feeding him special treats from the kitchen, entertaining him with chats and games. But Marty could no longer ignore her concerns. Surely Willie could not help but miss the attention that rightly should have been his.

In her growing anxiety, Marty took a walk, hardly knowing where to begin in her thinking to address the problem. Certainly Clark was loved in Missie's home. Willie had great respect for him. Missie loved him deeply, and the boys doted on their grandfather. Still, Willie's immediate family needed their own father and husband, and he needed Missie and their sons.

Marty wondered just how to discuss the issue with Clark. Would he see her concern and understand? What could they do? They were committed now to staying for the winter. And it wasn't possible to live in Missie's home and shut one's self away from the rest of the family.

At last Marty decided she must at least talk it over with Clark. If he did not see it as anything to get concerned about, then Marty, too, would try to put it from her mind.

That night after they had retired, Marty hesitantly broached the subject. She hoped Clark wouldn't think she was just being foolish, making mountains out of molehills.

"I've been thinkin'," said Marty slowly from her side of the bed. "It must be rather difficult fer Willie with us here."

"Willie?"

"Well, it wouldn't be, normally. But now, with yer accident an' all."

"I try not to cut in on Willie's time," answered Clark. "I know he's a very busy man. I've even found a few little ways I've been able to help lately."

"Oh, Willie ain't feelin' at all thet yer a loafer, thet ya aren't doin' yer share," assured Marty quickly. "I know thet. He's always tellin' me jest how special it is for 'im to have ya here. An' he tells me, too, of how ya been organizin' the corrals an' fixin' up his barn."

"Yer talkin' 'bout his family, then?"

"Ya mean —"

"I've been thinkin' on it, too. Missie frets over me far too much. It's done in love, an' I 'preciate it, but it don't leave her much time fer payin' attention to her husband — to the boys, too. I love the little tykes very dearly. But they're gittin' so's they come to me when they scratch a knee or pound a finger."

"You've noticed!" exclaimed Marty, very relieved.

"I've noticed. An' now thet you've noticed, it won't be near so hard fer me to make the suggestion I been thinkin' on."

"Suggestion?"

"Well, we can't jest up an' pull out now. They do need us to git thet little church started. We can't leave 'em now, Marty."

Marty agreed with a nod.

"An' it don't seem too smart to be carryin' on here in the same household as Willie an' Missie. Two families in the same house for very long — especially when one of 'em is the grandparents — often don't work so good."

"So?" Marty queried.

251

"So I think it's 'bout time fer a move."

"A move? Now where could we move? Yer not thinkin' of goin' into thet wild town —"

Clark stopped her with a laugh. "No, no wild town."

"Then —"

"The soddy."

"The . . . the *soddy?*" Marty was incredulous.

"Why not? Willie and Missie lived in it fer two winters, an' they had Nathan at the time. Surely you an' me could make do fer one winter. Jest the two of us. I've been thinkin' it might even be kinda fun." He grinned and said, "Would be like the old days in our little cabin back when we . . ."

Marty's expression must have slowed him down for a bit, but then he went on, "I've been checkin' it over, an' the walls are sturdy, the windows in place. The roof looks real good. Guess Willie jest had a new one put on to humor Missie fer our comin' out here. No reason a'tall why we couldn't be nice an' comfy fer the winter there."

Marty's initial aversion to the idea began to soften. She laughed softly. "Well, I never dreamed I'd be livin' in a soddy. An' at my age!"

"Ya keep referrin' to yer age," said Clark. "I'm not about to consider myself married to an old woman, so ya jest better stop sayin' it."

Marty laughed again.

"Well," prompted Clark. "What 'bout the soddy? Ya willin'? It still has the furniture — such as it is."

"Why not?" said Marty, lifting her shoulders in a shrug. "Think of all the time I'll have jest to sit an' read or sew. Not much to keepin' a soddy up."

"Sounds like a woman of leisure," Clark commented. "But ya know I'll at least be expectin' as good care as I've got here —" But he couldn't finish the thought since Marty was throwing her pillow at him.

"Then it's settled," he said when they'd finished laughing. "We'll move in first thing tomorra."

"Don't ya think Missie might need some time to think on the idea?"

"She'll git used to it. Ya give her time an' she might jest think of all kinds'a reasons why we shouldn't."

"Maybe yer right," agreed Marty. "All right, we'll move tomorra, then."

She kissed Clark and turned over to go to sleep. In the darkness, a smile played around her lips. She and Clark were going to live in a soddy! Wouldn't her friends back home think that was something else? Well, she'd have her share of experiences to tell them, that was for sure. She could hardly wait to write the next letter back home to the children. Imagine that — she and Clark living in a soddy!

FIFTEEN
MOVING

The next morning at the breakfast table, Nathan was busy shoving in Wong's muffins by the mouthful and making plans for himself and his grandfather for the day.

"An' we can ride over to the big hill an' look right over the range to where all the hands will be drivin' the cattle. We can see 'em start off on the trail drive to the town market. An' —"

"Whoa, cowboy," said Clark. "Thet shore sounds like a lot of fun all right, but I'm afraid I can't be runnin' off today. Fact is, I was thinkin' of askin' fer yer help today."

Nathan looked at his grandfather with surprise and interest. "Sure, Grandpa. I'll help ya."

Josiah cut in. "Me he'p G'an'pa."

"You're too little," Nathan answered with big-brother assurance, but Clark was quick to encourage the younger boy. "Shore ya can help. We're gonna need all the hands we can git."

Josiah beamed at being included.

"What're you up to?" asked Missie.

"Yer ma and me decided to move today."

"Move?"

"Yep."

"Stop your teasing, Pa," said Missie.

"Not jokin' around, daughter. Never been more serious."

"Then what do you mean, 'move'?"

"Well, we decided it might be kinda fun to spend the winter in the soddy."

"You *are* joking!" Missie obviously could not believe Clark was serious.

"No, I'm not."

"Whyever would you do that?"

"Why not? The soddy is snug and warm and big enough fer the two of us. It would be an adventure to talk about when we git back home."

"Oh, Pa," said Missie, exasperation in her voice. "Don't talk about anything so silly."

"Little girl," said Clark firmly, "it's not silly and I really am serious 'bout this."

Missie turned to Marty. "Tell me he's only teasing."

"No," said Marty matter-of-factly. "He's not. We talked it over last night. We decided it would be better fer all of us if we lived

separate fer the winter. We'll be right nearby
—"

"I don't understand one word of what you're sayin'," Missie said, rising from her chair with her face white and set. "If you're serious, I'd like to know why. Haven't we been caring for you — ?"

Clark quickly interrupted her. "My dear," he said gently, "ya shore as the world have been doin' everythin' fer me . . . an fer yer ma. An' we 'preciate it . . . more'n we ever could say. But now thet I'm gittin' about an' am able to mostly care fer myself, well, yer ma an' me think it's 'bout time yer family had ya back again . . . all to themselves."

Willie's eyes widened with understanding, then he lowered his gaze. Marty knew he would say nothing, but she also knew he was aware now of their observations about the situation in his home.

"That's silly," Missie continued to fume. "My family has had me all along. Never have I been more than a few feet away from any of them. Why, they always knew right where to find me. We've *loved* having you here. Besides, it was all because you came to visit us that you lost that leg —"

"Missie," Clark interrupted again, "I don't want to ever hear ya say thet I lost my leg because I came here. It coulda happened at home jest as well as here. The place has nothin' to do with it, an' I never want ya to feel any kind of guilt or responsibility thet the accident happened because I was here."

"Well," Missie said, lowering her eyes but seeming to brush aside Clark's comment with her gesture, "I won't feel guilt — I promise — but I still don't understand your wanting to move on out. We've so enjoyed having you here. Before we know it, the winter will be over and you'll be off home again. We want you here as much as possible. Tell them, Willie," she implored her husband. But Willie merely continued eating his scrambled eggs and muffins.

"Tell them, Willie," Missie instructed again.

Willie swallowed and looked from one to the other. It was apparent that he did not wish to be involved in the discussion. Clark spoke up before Willie was obliged any further.

"We know our son-in-law would never suggest we leave his home an' his table, Missie. We really want to do this, not because we are not welcome here, but because we feel it would be good fer all of us. We'll be right nearby and can come in fer coffee whenever we need a stroll. Yer ma will be over often to borrow cups of sugar and talk 'womenfolk talk.' The boys can come an' visit us in the soddy." Clark winked. "It could be jest a heap of fun. Marty an' I have never lived all by ourselves, ya know."

"And nothing I can say will make you change your mind?" Missie said, her one last effort at persuasion.

" 'Fraid not. Iffen the winter gits too tough an' we begin to get cold, we might come crawlin' back beggin' to be 'llowed in," said Clark lightly.

"I'll let ya in, Grandpa," assured Nathan, and everyone began to laugh.

"I let ya in, G'an'pa," echoed Josiah, not wanting to be outdone.

Missie moved for the coffeepot. "Well, if you are determined to do it, I guess I can't stop you, but I still don't like it."

"Look, honey," said Marty, understanding how their daughter felt, "if we didn't think it for the best, we wouldn't do it. Honest! Just give it a chance, will you, Missie? If it doesn't seem to be working for the best of all concerned, we'll move back in here. All right?"

Missie brightened some and leaned over to kiss Marty on her forehead.

"I'm sorry. It just took me off guard." She managed a smile. "If you're sure that it's what you want, my soddy is all yours. But

I'm warning you, Mama, it can get awful cramped on a winter's day."

Marty laughed. "Well, I have an advantage you didn't have, my dear."

"Yes?" asked Missie.

"You," said Marty. "If I git to feelin' cramped, I can jest bundle up an' make a dash fer yer big, beautiful home. You didn't have a big house or a daughter nearby, so ya jest had to sit tight."

Missie smiled again. "Well, I hope you feel cramped real often," she said. "Then you'll visit me lots."

Clark put down his empty cup. "Well, fellas," he said to the boys, "guess we'd better git started with this here move. Got yerself a wagon we kin use?"

The boys scrambled down and led the way to the bedroom that had been known as Grandpa and Grandma's for the last few months. Clark followed, his crutch beating a rhythmic tattoo behind them.

"I'll see what I can find for rugs an' blankets," offered Missie. "You'll need some decent dishes, too. Those in the soddy are in bad shape."

"Now, don't ya fuss none," Marty warned her daughter, but she knew she might as well bid the sun not to shine. Missie was sure to fuss. Marty just shrugged her shoulders. Perhaps in the fussing Missie would find some fun. She followed Missie out, determined to make a real adventure for them all on this moving day.

The nights were cooler now, and the wood fire in the old cookstove made the snug little soddy cozy and warm. Clark had encouraged Marty to visit Missie often during the first few days after their move, to assure her that indeed they had not forsaken her. Marty also invited Missie down to the soddy for afternoon tea, and Missie's many memories of the primitive dwelling gave her parents a new understanding of their daughter's first years in the West. She told of her first shocking sight of the small grass-covered mound that was to be her home, and her horror at seeing from inside the dirt roof and dirt floor, and her feeling of fear as she laid Nathan on the bed lest the chunks of earth come tumbling down on top of the wee baby. She described their first Christmas and the cowboys sitting almost toe to toe, enjoying a simple Christmas dinner. She told of Cookie holding Baby Nathan when he had the croup and helping him to breathe freely again. She talked about her first visit from Maria, her difficulty in drying her wash, her cooped-up feelings. But all the time she talked there was nostalgia in her voice, and her deep affection for the little soddy showed. Marty even began to wonder if Missie might be envying them the chance to live in it!

The boys loved to come, and Marty and Clark found themselves listening for their knock on the door and the two little voices calling, "Grandpa!" "Grandma!" They would pester Clark as he tried to study for the Sunday lessons. They coaxed to be able to add fuel to the fire. They wanted to roll on the bed, scratch marks in the dirt floor, and have their meals at the small table. They brought garden vegetables, fresh eggs, or milk from their mother. They even brought treats from Wong's kitchen.

Clark and Marty enjoyed them but always made sure they were home to greet their father when he returned at the end of the day.

Life finally had settled into a warm, comfortable, wholesome routine for all of them. Marty was thankful that Clark had proposed the move, feeling that it truly was better for all concerned. Willie looked less tense, more relaxed and happy, as well. He had needed to be master in his own home again. Even Missie took on a new glow. The past months had drained all of them, but now it was time for life to return to normal.

Marty sat in front of the soddy, knitting and soaking in the late fall sun; Clark came around the corner, expertly managing his crutch and a pail of spring water. He set the pail down and sank into a chair beside Marty, wiping his brow.

His chuckle brought Marty's head up. *Now what is he findin' so funny?* she asked herself and then repeated it to Clark.

"Nothin's funny, really. Jest thinkin' thet God really *does* make 'all things work together fer good.' "

"Meanin'?"

"This here leg — the one I ain't got no more. Ya notice which one is missin'?"

"Yah, the left one."

"Yep, the left one — but more'n thet. Look, it frees up my right hand when I'm workin'. See, I use the crutch in the left. Not only thet, but it's the left one I chopped into thet winter takin' out logs. Remember?"

Marty wondered how he thought she could forget. She still went weak and sick inside when she thought of how Clark had returned to the house with his pale face and blood-drenched foot. "I remember," she said, her voice tight.

"Well, thet's the foot thet's gone. Thet ras-

cal has kept me awake more'n one night —
'specially when the weather's 'bout to
change."

"You never mentioned thet before."

"Weren't no reason to. Guess it won't
keep me awake again, though."

Clark chuckled again. Marty couldn't
quite bring herself to join him, but she
smiled at this strong, patient man of hers
who saw God's hand in all the circumstances of his life.

Clark had a visit from Juan. It had been
three weeks since they had seen the de la
Rosas. They had been informed that Juan
and Maria had gone away, and they assumed Juan was still gathering equipment
and supplies for his medical practice. He
greeted Clark now with a firm handshake
and clear eyes. Marty sensed that he wanted
to talk to Clark in private and left the two
of them alone over steaming cups of coffee.

"Well, after much prayer and struggle,"
began Juan immediately, "I did as you rec-
ommended."

"You have been home?"

"I have been home," Juan said with deep
feeling.

"I'm glad," said Clark. "An' how did yer
pa receive you?"

Juan's eyes clouded for a moment. "My father, I am sorry to say, was not there to greet me. He died seven months ago."

"I'm sorry," Clark said with sincerity.

"I am sorry, too. I should have gone sooner. I should not have let stubborn pride keep me away."

"An' yer mother?"

"My mother welcomed me with outstretched arms."

Clark smiled. "I'm sure she did."

"My father had died and left my mother all alone. Daily she prayed that if her son Juan was still living he would come back to her. Because of my foolishness, it took a long time for my mother's prayers to be answered."

"We are all foolish at times," Clark reminded him.

Juan went on. "My mother could scarcely believe her eyes when I walked into her room. She had failed much. She did not eat well or care for herself since my father died. When she saw me, she wept long for joy. Then she told me how my father had pined after sending me away. He tried for many months to find me — to ask for my forgiveness — but there was no trace of where I had gone. Before he died, he had my mother promise that she would keep trying. She did. She sent out men and offered rewards, but she could not find me."

Juan stopped to wipe a hand across his eyes. "I caused them much hurt," he murmured.

"Ya didn't know."

"No, I didn't know. I was too busy nursing hurts of my own. . . . My mother was so happy to hear that I am a doctor again. I would like you to meet her."

"I'd love to meet her. Maybe someday —"

"Not someday. Now."

"Ya mean — ?"

"She's here. I left her up at the house having tea with Missie and Maria. She wants very much to meet the man who sent her son home to her."

"But I . . . *I* didn't do thet. Ya went on yer own. It was yer decision."

"Yes, you let me make the decision. You left me my dignity. But you knew when you talked to me how I would have to decide." Juan smiled.

"I'd love to meet yer mama," said Clark, picking up his crude crutch.

"An' I have something for you," said Juan, returning to the door and reaching outside for a carefully fashioned crutch with a padded arm bar. "They can make very good crutches in the city," he added.

Clark took the new crutch and handled it carefully, looking over every angle and the total length of it.

"It's a dandy," he grinned. "An' I thank ya."

Clark, with his new "store-bought" crutch, and Juan went to the house together. Juan explained as they walked, "My mother had no desire to live alone on the rancho. As I did not wish to return to ranching in that area, we decided to sell the ranch to the man who has run it for my father. Mother is insisting on using much of the money from the sale for my medical practice. She wants us to have good equipment for those who need help. She is going to live with us. We are all so happy. Maria can't remember having a mother. Hers died when she was a very young girl. We are all very happy, Mr. Clark, and we thank you."

Señora de la Rosa was a delicate, dark woman with flashing eyes and a quick smile. In spite of her years and the intense sorrow in her past, she still had a youthful spirit and vibrant outlook on life. Clark and Marty liked her immediately.

"Mama has said that we shall all come to service together," said Maria. "When God works to answer her prayers through people who worship — even though they worship

267

in a different way than she is used to — they must have the approval of God, she says. And so God would also surely approve of us worshiping together with them. So we shall be here next Sunday — and all the Sundays — and we will be glad to help in the building of the new church."

The prayer time together before the de la Rosas left for home was full of fervent thanksgiving to God.

SIXTEEN
WINTER

Nathan celebrated his sixth birthday — a big event for him at any time, but even more important on this occasion because his grandparents were there to help in the merrymaking. The Kleins and de la Rosas also came for the event, and the house rang with laughter and friendly chatter.

Josiah got his full share of attention on the occasion, coming in from the kitchen wrapped in one of Wong's big white aprons. Everyone had a good laugh, and Joey was pleased with the response.

Nathan had insisted he wanted a crutch "jest like Grandpa's" for his birthday and could not understand the objections to getting him one. He wanted to imitate his grandfather in every way, and he felt that the use of a crutch — even though he planned on keeping his leg — would be one more thing he could share with this man he loved so dearly. Missie was horrified at the thought of such a thing, fearing that Nathan's toting about a crutch might be tempting fate. She tried to talk Nathan out of it, promising him all kinds of things in its place. But he still wanted one. Clark finally had a man-to-man talk with the boy, and Nathan came away from the discussion happy that he had two good legs to walk on "like his pa."

Willie was pleased with the profits from the fall cattle sale, and he and Missie left by train for a larger city to do some shopping. Clark and Marty took charge of the two boys while the LaHayes were gone. The children begged to sleep in the soddy with their grandparents, and the four had a cozy and enjoyable time together.

The shipment of furnishings eventually arrived, and Missie now had a new dining room — splendid in its dark wood furniture, thick rug, and rich draperies. Marty complimented Missie many times on her excellent taste, but Missie laughed and replied that anyone could have good taste as long as they had good money.

Missie, too, had a birthday. Marty thoroughly enjoyed the chance to make the cake and prepare the birthday dinner after the number of years they had been apart for this event. All the ranch hands were invited for the meal. The large family dining room was almost as crowded as the little soddy had been many Christmases ago. But Missie loved it, and the cowboys all seemed to appreciate it, too.

Marty awoke one morning to the sound of the wind howling around the little soddy. The winter's first storm had moved in without warning. Clark was already up and had gotten a nice fire going before reading his Bible at the small table.

Marty snuggled under the covers again and thought about how fortunate they were. Winter might be here with all its sound and fury, but they were snug and warm and dry. Marty did not put off getting up for long. Clark had coffee perking, and the smell of it quickly enticed her from the bed. She crawled forth rather hesitantly, but the comforting heat from the fire meant the howling wind had no power in their warm shelter.

"My, thet coffee smells good! I think ya purposely made it jest to tempt me from the bed," she said, slipping her arms around Clark's shoulders and giving him a kiss on the cheek.

"Ya hear thet wind?" asked Clark. "Sounds

like we're gonna find out all 'bout a western winter."

"Guess we will at thet," said Marty, "but ya know, it ain't scarin' me none."

Clark merely smiled.

"Whatcha doin'?" asked Marty.

"Well, Henry figures thet when the storms strike on a Sunday, the folks from any distance won't be able to make it here fer the service. So we talked it over an' decided to make 'em up some lesson materials they could read and study at home."

"Thet's a good idea!" Marty enthused.

"At least this'll help 'em to feel a part of the group, even iffen they can't git here. They'll be studyin' the same portion of the Word as the rest of us."

"Thet's nice," Marty encouraged again.

"But I've been at this fer what seems ages already, an' I shore could do with breakfast. I was jest sittin' here thinkin' this is the kind of a mornin' I could use a nice big stack of pancakes."

Marty laughed and went to get dressed so she could make Clark his pancakes.

The winter weather continued as it had begun. The storms moved in and out of the area, leaving behind big drifts of snow. As predicted, the Sunday crowd at the La-

Hayes' diminished during that time. Henry saw to it that those members of the little congregation not able to attend received Clark's Sunday lesson materials.

The church building committee worked hard at drawing up plans and arranging for the materials for spring building. All the members of the group were anxious to get into their own little church. Juan's mother sent away to the city and ordered a bell for the spire. She felt that a church of God should have a bell for calling together the worshipers.

Donations for materials and labor came in from many of the neighbors. Willie and Henry were sure that when a building was finally in evidence, the Sunday attendance would increase sharply.

Cookie often dropped in at the soddy to see Clark. Marty was sure he waited until he saw her heading for Missie's for a chat or to do some baking together, and then, in her absence, he would hobble off to have a cup of coffee with Clark. Clark did not discuss much of their conversation with her — she knew he was honoring Cookie's desire for confidence. Yet she also realized the old cowboy was deeply troubled about his past life and its effect on his eternal future. Marty wanted to hasten "the awakening" and say outright to Cookie, "Yer a sinner an' ya realize yer bad deeds can keep ya from heaven. I was a sinner, too. But one needn't stay in thet state. Christ Jesus came so every person can be forgiven and restored to all that God intended when He created us. All ya need do, Cookie, is to accept the gift of life He offers to ya. It's jest thet simple. Nothin' to it at all. No need to fret an' stew over whether it's a good idea or a bad idea. Common sense tells ya thet ya can't lose on such a deal. Jest do it an' git it taken care of."

Clark was far more patient with the man, and Marty knew he would carefully explain what Scripture had to say about mankind's fall into sin — beginning with Adam and Eve — about human selfishness, about every person's need of a Savior, and about God's solution to this need. Cookie was gradually realizing his own need and understanding what Christ had done for him, Clark quietly told Marty. He felt confident that when Cookie made his decision, there would be no turning back. Still, Marty inwardly chafed, wishing it wouldn't take the man so long.

Scottie, too, was on the Davis' prayer list. They liked and respected the foreman, and they longed to see him make his peace with

God. Scottie came to the Sunday services whenever he was free to do so, but he did not seem to feel any need of a change in his life.

Lane, the one who had helped Doc de la Rosa with the surgery, was growing spiritually. Daily he sought out Clark or Willie for the answer to some question he had found as he read the Scriptures. He not only read the Bible, but he endeavored to live daily by its commands and precepts. Lane could never be accused of being a hypocrite. Even the bitter Smith began to show a grudging respect for Lane and one day admitted to Jake, "Don't hold much to religion. Always figured it was fer women an' young'uns an' men who couldn't stand on their own feet. But if I was ever to git religion, I'd want the kind thet Lane's got."

Jake looked skeptical. "Didn't know there was more'n one kind," he drawled.

"Ya didn't? Then ya ain't been watchin' Lane lately."

"So where did Lane git his special brand?" sneered Jake.

"Reckon he got it from the same place the boss an' his pa-in-law got theirs. It seems to be made of the same stuff."

Jake thought of Willie and his steadiness — even through the tough times — his fairness with his men, and his concern for his community. He also thought of Clark and his acceptance of his handicap, and he murmured under his breath, "Yah, reckon it is." Then he turned to Smith. "So, iffen they's able to pass it on an' are so anxious to share it, what's stoppin' ya from gittin' yerself some?"

Smith did not answer. He just scowled and rode away.

When Christmastime arrived, Marty's thoughts were often on her family at home, even as her thoughts had been on Missie during the Christmases they had been separated. Marty reminded herself that Kate was there to help Ellie make a Christmas for the family on the farm, and the last letter had stated that Nandry's and Clae's families would both be home for Christmas, as well. Soon after the new year, Joe and Clae and little Esther would be leaving for the city, where Joe would finally have the opportunity to get his seminary training. Marty wished she would be there to tell them good-bye, but it brought a certain joy to her heart to know they would be in the very city where Luke would eventually take his medical training. It would not be nearly so hard to let him go knowing that Clae and

Joe would be there to welcome him.

Even so, Marty thought much of her other family as she made her preparations for Christmas with the family in the West.

Wong and Cookie combined their efforts to prepare a Christmas feast for all the members of the ranch family. It was bound to be a sumptuous affair, and everyone was anticipating the occasion. Marty supposed they would all eat more than they really needed, but somehow even that spoke of God's abundant blessings to them, especially this Christmas.

Nathan and Josiah had worked themselves up into a fever of excitement. Nathan knew of Christmases past and the thrill of receiving gifts. Josiah was too young to remember other Christmases, but he was willing to take his big brother's word for what would happen.

Marty had busily knitted mittens, socks, and scarves for the two boys, and Clark had been carefully fashioning a snow sled. "Shore enough," he told Marty, "with all them hills around, there must be one that a sled would work good on." Marty heartily agreed. Even though they would be many days' journey away from the rest of their family, they were happy to spend this Christmas with Missie, Willie, and the boys.

On Christmas Eve, Marty finished the last of her Christmas presents, and they packed up their gifts and themselves and went out into the starlit winter night for the short trip to Missie's house. They had planned an evening of games, Christmas carols, and popcorn over the log fire. The gifts would be exchanged the next morning.

Nathan answered their knock and squealed his delight at their arrival, and Josiah was just behind him to echo his joy.

"Hi, Grandpa! Hi, Grandma! Come in. We're havin' Christmas," shouted Nathan.

"Ch'is'mas," echoed Josiah and pulled them in by the hands.

The evening was full of love and joy. They chatted and ate and played games and sang amid laughter and lighthearted banter. They shared their memories of other Christmases. Nathan loved the stories, but finally Josiah's lids started to droop as he fought to stay awake.

Finally Missie rose to put the two children to bed. Nathan certainly was not anxious to go, afraid that he might miss out on something. Missie assured him everything would be there for him to see and share in the morning.

When the children were settled for the night and the grown-ups were having coffee and slices of Wong's Christmas cake made from one of Marty's recipes, Missie, her cheeks aglow and her eyes alight, shared her secret.

"You are going to be grandparents again in July," she said. "We're going to have another little one."

"Oh, thet's wonderful!" cried Marty, hugging her girl close. "But, my, I wish it would be sooner! We should be off home long 'fore then, an' it will be so hard to leave without seein' him — or her."

"I'm hoping for a girl this time," admitted Missie. "But a boy would be all right, too. Willie's always needing lots of cowboys on the ranch." They laughed together, and Willie looked pleased.

They talked further about their hopes and dreams concerning the new baby. Marty noted how thankful she was that Dr. de la Rosa would be there for the birthing. And perhaps by then he would also have his little medical office ready for use.

Clark and Marty, arm in arm, returned over the snow-packed path back to the little soddy. They were just about to enter when Cookie appeared, hobbling hurriedly toward the bunkhouse from the cook shack, a small lantern swinging by his side. Marty assumed he must be going to meet with the cowboys for their own Christmas celebration, but Clark said there seemed to be an urgency to Cookie's steps.

"Somethin' wrong?" he called to Cookie.

Cookie hesitated. "No, nothin' wrong, really. Least not fer you to concern yourselves with. Scottie jest came ridin' in with some stray cowpoke he found out there on the range someplace. Fella's in pretty bad shape. Looks like he ain't et in a week, an' the weather's kinda on the cold side to be sittin' out under a rock outcroppin'. Lane, he went over to see what the doc would advise fer his frostbite."

Cookie was about to move on, but Clark called to him, "I'll join ya. Don't s'pose there be much I can do, but I'll take a look-see."

He turned to Marty and spoke softly, "Ya go on in out of this cold to bed. I'll jest be a few minutes an' then I'll be in to join ya. Ya might want to check on the fire again 'fore ya turn in."

Then Clark deftly hopped along after Cookie, his crutch making strange tracks in the fresh snow.

The cowboys had put the unfortunate man to bed, Lane directing them to his bunk before he left for the doctor's. Smithie was using the only medicine he was ac-

280

quainted with — a shot of whiskey. The man was sputtering and fussing, so Clark knew at least he was alive.

"Where'd ya find 'im?"

"Scottie found him someplace out there. Didn't even have a horse. Said it had died. He was walkin' somewhere — who knows where — an' the bad weather caught him. He tried to hole up in a sheltered spot and wait out the wind. He coulda been there till spring and not had the wind stop none."

Clark smiled in spite of his concern. "Is he in bad shape?"

"Don't know yet. He has some frostbite fer sure, an' he's thin as a rattler. 'Bout as mean as one, too, I'm thinkin'. All he can do is cuss an' name call. Don't seem to 'preciate much the trouble Scottie took fer 'im."

Clark moved nearer to the bed.

The man before him was heavily bearded and his eyes were only dark holes in his head. Bedraggled and dirty, he looked as though he hadn't had a meal in weeks. Yet something about him was vaguely familiar.

Clark motioned for them to move the lantern in closer, the result being a gruff complaint and a curse from the stranger. Clark looked steadily into the thin, shadowed face and finally was sure.

"Jedd," he said, shaking his head in disbelief. "Jedd Larson."

Seventeen
Jedd

The sick man stirred slightly and mumbled something incoherent. All other eyes in the room turned on Clark.

"Ya know this man?" asked Scottie.

"It's Jedd Larson; there's shore no mistakin' thet. But he do look in bad shape. Last I seen 'im he was still young and strong — and a mite on the stubborn side. Marty an' me raised his two girls — though it's hard fer us to remember at times they ain't really our own flesh and blood. We think of 'em as such."

"Well, I'll be a —" exclaimed Cookie, though he was not allowed to finish his statement, for the ill man began to toss and call out in his delirium. Clark leaned over him in an effort to understand what the man was saying. He straightened as he caught the one word that was repeated over and over. Jedd was saying, "Tina."

"Understand 'im?" asked Cookie.

"He's askin' fer his wife. She's been gone fer a number of years now. Can't say thet Jedd treated her too kindly whilst she was here. Maybe he's regrettin' it now."

Clark reached out a hand and felt Jedd's brow, hot with fever. He leaned over the man again and spoke his name softly. There was no response. Clark knelt down beside the bed and took the man's hand in his. He began to talk to Jedd. The cowboys gradually moved back from the bed to allow the two men a degree of privacy.

"Jedd," Clark said clearly, "Jedd, this is Clark. Clark Davis, yer neighbor. Remember me, Jedd? Clark Davis. Clark and Marty. Ya left yer girls with us, Jedd, when ya decided to go west. Tina wanted 'em to have school-in'. Tina asked Marty to give the girls a chance, Jedd. Remember? They are fine girls, Jedd, yer Nandry an' Clae. You'd be mighty proud of 'em. Both of 'em married. Nandry has a family of four. An' Clae's got a little girl. Yer a grandpa, Jedd. A grandpa five times over. You'd be proud of yer grand-children, too, could ya see 'em."

The man was not responding. He stared off into space and now and then mumbled or cursed as the warmth of the room in-creased the pain in his frozen limbs. Clark continued to speak to him, rubbing his hand as he spoke, careful not to touch the frost-bitten fingers.

"Jedd, Nandry and Clae still worry 'bout ya. Still pray fer ya daily. They want ya back, Jedd. They want to share with ya their love, their family, their God. Remember, Jedd? Tina found peace with God before she died. Well, yer girls are servin' their mother's God, too, Jedd. There's nothin' they would like better than fer you to know God, too. Ya hear me, Jedd? Yer girls love ya. Nandry an' Clae — they love ya. Tina loved ya, an' God loves ya, too, Jedd.

"Ya gotta keep holdin' on," Clark continued, speaking softly but with urgency. "Ya can't jest go an' give up now. Hang in there, Jedd."

There was hardly a pause in the low murmur of Clark's voice until Lane and the doctor arrived. Dr. de la Rosa examined Jedd carefully and gave him some medication. He shook his head as he turned to Clark and the waiting ranch hands.

"He is in bad shape. He was not well even before he was caught in the storm."

"Will he make it?" asked Clark.

"I do not know."

"Please, Doc," said Clark, "iffen there's anything at all you can do fer 'im — anything to bring him through — I'll stand the bill. This here is the father of two girls Marty an' me raised as our own. He's been bullheaded and stubborn, thoughtless and sometimes cruel, but his girls love 'im. If only Jedd can live long enough fer someone to tell 'im of God's love an' fergiveness. Thet would mean so much to his girls . . . to us. Ya think you can bring him round, Doc? I jest can't bear the thought of 'im dyin' without my bein' able to talk with him 'bout his girls and 'bout God's love for 'im."

Dr. de la Rosa looked very solemn. "I can only try," he said. "You pray that God might work a miracle."

The doctor no doubt thought Clark would go to his little soddy and kneel in prayer, but Clark saw the need as imminent. He immediately knelt beside the bed on which Jedd lay and began to pray fervently for a miracle. Around him feet shuffled as cowboys, uncertain of what to do, shifted position. But Lane knew. He crossed to the bunk and knelt down beside Clark, joining him in his prayer.

"Dear God," began Clark, "you know this here man before us. He's been sinful, God, but so have we all. He's made some bad judgments, but so have we. He needs ya, Lord, just as we all do. He has never recognized you as God an' Savior, an' he needs thet chance, Lord. He can't hear or respond in his present condition, so we need ya to do a miracle, Lord, an' help the doc bring him round so we can talk with him and read yer Word so he might have the chance to decide fer himself. We are askin' this, Lord, in the name of Jesus, yer Son, who died so each one of us — includin' Jedd here — could have life eternal. Thank ya, Lord, for hearin' the prayer of those of us who bow before ya. Amen."

Clark stood up, adjusting his crutch to support himself. The man before him still lay unconscious.

Lane reached out and touched the whiskered cheek. Then he turned to the doctor. "What's next, Doc?"

Juan looked back at the man on the bed. "I think I should take him to my home. I can put him on the cot in the office."

All eyes looked at the doctor, questioning.

The doctor continued. "He is going to need much care. We can watch him there. It will make my mother feel needed. She wishes to do something for someone, and this will be her chance. If I am able to help this man . . ." Juan hesitated, then continued. "I think it is too late to save many of his fingers and toes. Perhaps he will lose them all."

It was sobering news. Clark noticed some of the hands in the room unconsciously curl up into fists, as though defying fate to try to take their own.

Lane moved first. "Ya want me to git a team?" he asked the doctor.

"Yes. Put lots of hay in the bottom of a wagon. We'll need to make him a bed."

For the second time that Christmas Eve, Lane made the trip to the doctor's, this time driving the team that carried a critically ill man. His saddle horse tied to the rear, Dr. de la Rosa rode in the wagon with them, watching Jedd to be sure he stayed well covered in the bitter winter wind.

Clark returned to the little soddy and found that Marty had not gone to bed.

"I've been frettin' an' thinkin' all kinds of things," she said.

"You'll never believe this," said Clark, "but maybe you should sit down fer this. Thet man Scottie brought in off the range is Jedd Larson."

"Jedd?"

"Shore ain't in very good shape."

"Oh, Clark. Did ya tell 'im 'bout his girls? Did he say — ?"

"Jedd didn't say much 'ceptin' a few cuss words, Marty. He is plumb outta his head. No, thet's not right. He did say one thing.

Over an' over. He said 'Tina.' "

"Tina . . . then he remembers."

"Somehow thet one name gave me hope, Marty. Somehow it helped me to believe this wasn't jest fate thet sent Jedd this way, but God givin' him a chance to find *Him*."

"Oh, Clark, I pray it might be so," said Marty, tears filling her eyes.

"If only I could have talked to him — made him understand me somehow."

"Can I see 'im?" asked Marty.

"He's gone."

"Gone? But how could —"

"Lane went fer Dr. de la Rosa, an' the doc decided when he checked Jedd out it would be better fer 'im to have Jedd at his house so he could watch over 'im. Lane took 'im on over in the wagon. They left jest a few minutes ago."

"Oh, Clark. I hope he makes it. I hope ya have a chance to talk to him. Was he really bad, Clark?"

Clark nodded his head solemnly.

"Oh, Clark!" cried Marty again. "Let's pray." The two knelt beside the bed and prayed long and fervently for this one from the past with such strong ties to their family.

"Please, Lord, bring him round enough to understand ya love him in spite of what he's done to his wife, to his girls," Marty prayed. "Help us know how to show him thet love."

In spite of their shock and anxiety over Jedd, Christmas Day was a time of thanksgiving and joy. With two small boys in the house, it was impossible not to feel the excitement and pleasure of this celebration of Jesus' birth. Even though they had retired late the night before and had had difficulty getting to sleep, Clark and Marty were up early and over in the big house. Nathan and Josiah were already up and filling the house with cries of happiness as they looked at the gifts under the tree that had arrived sometime during the night. They did not seem very interested in their breakfast that morning.

Nathan was thrilled with the sled that Clark had made and begged to go out and try it even before he had eaten. Clark laughed and promised the boys he would take them out on the sled just as soon as their mother approved. Missie, smiling, shrugged her shoulders and shook her head.

Nathan's favorite gift from his parents was a new halter for Spider, his pony. Willie finally gave in to his pleadings and told him they would go to the barn and make sure the halter fit. Nathan soon reappeared, bundled to his eyebrows with Marty's gift of socks, mittens, and carelessly looped scarf. Willie laughed at the sight.

"Ya shore enough look well cared fer weatherwise, 'cept fer yer feet. Ain't ya plannin' to wear any boots?"

"They won't go over my big socks," replied Nathan, which brought more laughs.

Josiah soon rounded the corner, too. Still in his nightclothes, he also had looped his long scarf over it all. One eye was hidden and he peeked out from the other one, his head tipped to give him better vision. His mittens had been pulled onto the wrong hands, and the empty thumbs stuck out to the sides like two misplaced horns. The socks, partly on but mostly off, gave Josiah the appearance of duck feet. He waddled forward, pleased with himself and ready to join his brother and pa for the trip to the barn.

Now Willie really laughed. He led the two boys back to their room, properly dressed Josiah and helped Nathan to find socks and boots that worked together. Then, with the small Josiah on his pa's shoulders and Nathan trudging along at his side with the cherished new halter, Clark joined them and they all started out for the barn.

"They do make some sight, don't they?" said Missie at the window, her voice full of emotion.

"Don't know how many times I've stood at my window an' watched yer pa an' his sons crossin' the yard," Marty responded. "If I had no other reason to love yer pa than thet single one — the seein' of his care fer his young'uns — it would be enough to make me love him as long as God grants me breath," she continued softly.

They turned back to the preparations for the day. There was much to be done, for Christmas dinner for all of the hands had become a tradition on the LaHaye ranch. Though usually busy and going many different directions, on Christmas Day they took the time to all eat together and hear the reading of the Christmas story.

Around the morning's breakfast table, the discussion often returned to the wonder at Jedd Larson turning up on the LaHaye ranch. They had not heard of Jedd since he had left his farm back home and headed west so many years ago. Marty wished there was some way she could tell Clae and Nandry the exciting news, and then she remembered that if Jedd did not make it through this Christmas Day, the news they would have to share with their girls would be bad news, not good news. Again and again throughout the day Marty quietly prayed.

■ ■ ■ ■

After the trip to the barn, as promised, Clark took the boys for a sled ride.

At first it was difficult for him to pull the sled with the two small passengers up the nearby slope, but eventually he found that his crutch, jammed into the snow, made a good replacement for the limb he did not have.

The boys squealed with delight as Clark shoved them off and they made the short, swift trip down the hill. This time, Nathan pulled the sled back up the hill, but it was hard for little Josiah to climb back up through the deep snow on his own. Clark went to meet him and carried him up the hill piggyback. Again and again the two sped down the hill and made their slow and awkward climb back up. At last, exhausted but happy, they agreed to head back to the house and get warmed up.

"We'll have to do this again, huh, Grandpa?" said Nathan.

" 'G'in," echoed his little brother.

"Shore will," puffed Clark, who had enjoyed it almost as much as the boys.

"After dinner?" asked Nathan.

"Well, I dunno 'bout thet. I think I might

jest have to catch my breath a bit. And maybe yer pa an' ma might have some of their own plans fer after dinner."

"After thet, then?"

"We'll see," laughed Clark. "We'll see."

About one o'clock the cowboys began to arrive, kicking the snow from their boots and slapping their wide-brimmed hats against their sides. They laughed and joked as they filed in. Marty stood back in amazement as they stopped in the large entry and removed their boots and lined them up neatly against the wall, no doubt thinking of possible damage to Missie's fine rugs. Marty had been west only for a short while, but already she understood how important boots were to the ranch hands, how important it was not to be caught with your boots off. She smiled her appreciation for their thoughtfulness. But they seemed embarrassed and ill at ease as they stood looking down at their stockinged feet. Marty noticed that some of the socks had holes in them and wondered if she would dare offer to darn them. She said nothing now but went to the kitchen to find a worn towel. One by one she picked up the boots and carefully wiped away all traces of water and dirt. Then she handed them, pair by pair, back to the owners. The cowboys climbed back into the boots with warm grins and eloquent nods of thanks. They were now anticipating the meal that already was filling the air with delightful aromas as Wong carried dish after dish to the large dining room.

Before the meal, Willie, as the head of the home and the owner of the ranch, read to them the story of the birth of the Christ child. Some throats were self-consciously cleared and many gazes were fastened on the tops of boots or the big leathery hands in their laps, but everyone listened carefully. Willie then asked Clark to lead them in prayer.

The meal began in comparative silence, but it wasn't long until hearty laughter and good-natured teasing took over. Nathan and Josiah joined in merrily, describing in detail to the ranch hands their gifts of the morning, the trip to the barn with the new halter that "Spider liked real good," and their ride on Grandpa's sled.

After they all had eaten as much as they possibly could, the guests moved to the living room, where a friendly fire welcomed them. Henry was not there to lead them with his guitar, having decided to follow the LaHaye tradition and have a family Christmas dinner for his own hands. But in spite of the absence of Henry, they sang the

Christmas carols under Willie's direction. Those who did not sing seemed to enjoy listening.

Scottie was the first who had to leave. He always took responsibility for the Christmas shift with the cattle. Usually one or two of the other hands joined him voluntarily out of respect for their boss. Today it was Jake and Charlie. Lane announced that he planned to ride over to the doctor's to see how Jedd was doing. Clark said that he would like to go with him.

The cowboys left, calling their thanks as they flipped their Stetsons back on their heads.

After dinner, the two boys were tucked in for a much-needed nap. Missie and Marty went to help Wong and Cookie clear the dishes, and the house again fell into silence.

Clark and Lane saddled up for a visit to the doc's house and Jedd. The ride through the crisp afternoon felt particularly cold, and Clark especially noticed it in the stump of his missing leg. He had not thought to provide extra protection for the area, not realizing how sensitive it was to the temperature. Lane, without saying anything, swung down from his horse and pulled a blanket from behind his saddle. Speaking of other things, he crossed to Clark's horse and tucked the blanket around the stump, making sure it was fastened securely in place and would not slip with the movement of horse and rider. Still making no reference to the missing leg or the blanket, he remounted and they moved on. Clark was much more comfortable during the remainder of the ride.

They found Jedd in much the same condition as he had been the night before. Juan's mother sat with him. Jedd had been bathed, and his beard and hair had been neatly trimmed. His feet and hands bore large bandages, and Clark was reminded of the doctor's concern for the fingers and toes that had been frozen. When the two visitors found Jedd unconscious, they did not stay long. Juan promised that if the man roused, he would send one of his ranch hands with the message. The doctor seemed encouraged that Jedd had held his own throughout the day. His pulse rate had improved, and this gave Juan some hope.

Lane and Clark left for home after sharing a cup of hot coffee and some of Maria's special Christmas goodies.

As they mounted their horses, Clark tucked Lane's blanket around himself. "Never knowed," he said simply, "jest how much the cold would bother a leg like mine. Here I was pridin' myself thet I wouldn't suffer any cold toes on this side."

Lane smiled but only said, "It'll toughen."

EIGHTEEN
FROM DEATH TO LIFE

It was three days before a rider came from the de la Rosas' to inform them that Jedd Larson was now awake. Clark immediately saddled a horse and prepared to go to him. He tucked his Bible inside his jacket and asked Marty for an extra blanket.

"It's a trick I learned from Lane," explained Clark in answer to her unasked question. "This here short leg gets awful cold. A blanket keeps it more livable."

Marty spent the day knitting and praying. It seemed like Clark was gone forever, but at last Marty heard the sound of a horse approaching the barn. In the clear, crisp winter air, the sounds of the hoofbeats rang out clearly. Max left the yard on the run, always the first to welcome a rider.

Marty watched from the window until Clark came in sight, and then she grabbed her shawl and ran to meet him.

"Come to Missie's," she called. "She'll

want to hear all 'bout it, too."

Clark changed direction and headed for the big house as Marty ran down the rutted snow-packed path to meet him there.

"Oh, I was hoping you'd come right on over here," Missie called to them from the doorway. "I just couldn't wait to hear all about it."

Missie led the way to the open fire. "We're nearly bursting," she spoke for both of them. "Tell us about it quick."

"Did Jedd know ya this time?" Marty began.

"Oh, he knew me all right. Was almost as surprised to see me as I was to see him the other night."

"What did he say?"

"He asked first thing 'bout the girls."

Marty felt her throat constrict with emotion. "I'm so glad he cares somethin' fer 'em," she said.

"He seemed right concerned. Said he'd 'bout made up his mind to go on home. He was tryin' to reach town an' the train station when he got lost in the snow an' was stranded out on the range."

"Did he mention Tina again?"

"We talked 'bout Tina quite a piece."

Marty could wait no longer. "Clark," she said, "were ya able to talk to 'im 'bout his need fer God?"

"I was. We went through the main points in the Bible — from creation to redemption to Christ's return."

"Did he understand?"

"Seemed to."

"Did he . . . did he . . . ?"

Clark put his arm around Marty and pulled her close. His voice sounded husky as he said, "Those girls of ours are gonna be happy to know their pa joined with their ma today."

"Ya mean — ?"

"Jedd Larson made his peace with his Savior."

"Oh, thank ya, Father," prayed Marty aloud, happy tears running down her cheeks.

Clark cleared his throat.

"He joined Tina in another way, too." He paused for a moment, then said quietly, "Jedd didn't make it. Juan had to operate. Jedd wasn't strong enough to stand it. The frozen fingers and toes had turned bad, an' there weren't any way Juan could save 'im. He's been stayin' with him day an' night, fightin' to bring 'im through this, but —"

"But he did, Clark. He did!" exclaimed Marty. "Because of Juan's fight to save 'im, Jedd not only has life — but *everlastin'* life."

301

"I'm afraid it's hard for a doctor to look at things thet way," said Clark soberly.

"But it's true. And, oh, Clark, if you hadn't been here, Jedd maybe wouldn'ta decided to make his peace with God 'fore he died." Marty's eyes fell to Clark's pant leg, pinned up securely just below the knee. "If it weren't fer the accident, ya wouldn't still be here, Clark. We would've gone home long ago."

Clark pulled her closer to him and kissed her hair, and Missie joined them on the other side as they embraced and thanked the Lord together for Jedd's salvation.

During the long winter days, Marty spent much of her time in the little soddy knitting, mending, or hand-sewing for Missie and her family. She also had a basketful of socks to mend for the ranch hands, having made discreet inquiries after the boots had come off at dinnertime on Christmas. Clark used his hours to make things with his hands and his limited tools. In the long evenings, he spent hours with the Bible, preparing the Sunday lessons for the congregation.

Each Sunday after the worshipers gathered together for their service, there were discussions concerning the materials and the progress of the church building. As the committee continued planning and ordering supplies, the building was taking shape on paper and in the minds of the people, even though not a stake had been pounded or a nail driven. However, the supplies were all being stockpiled at the Newtons' as they arrived by train, and a building bee was planned as soon as the weather would permit. Folks hoped for an early spring so the work might be started.

As the weather improved, so did the Sunday attendance. Once again, the folks from the town ventured out on their long drive. But they seemed anxious to be a part of the fellowship and to keep informed about progress on the church building. Besides, they reported, though they enjoyed the Bible studies at home and it had been a good idea, it was not the same as meeting with the group and hearing Clark's insights on the truths from the Scripture portion.

During the week, when Marty felt too confined, she would toss a shawl about her shoulders and hurry over the snow-crusted path to Missie's house. On a few occasions, Missie came to visit her while the children slept. Missie said she loved to sit in the quiet, snug little soddy, sipping tea and telling stories about those first years at the ranch. Missie occasionally acknowledged aloud that the days were quickly passing and her beloved mother would all too soon return back home.

As the winter days lengthened, their visits turned to garden plans and setting hens. It was hard to stay in the house with the drifts of snow shrinking daily. The boys gamboled about like young colts finally set free in the sunshine and hints of warmth to come. Their mother had to coax and scold them to keep their warm jackets on and buttoned.

Clark, too, had been planning ahead, only his thoughts had taken a different turn. He thought often about the small congregation. He had enjoyed the opportunity to lead them over the winter months. He knew they were not likely to soon find a minister for the group. What would happen when he had to leave for home? Clark decided to ride over and talk about it with Henry. And so it was that Clark began to have study sessions with Henry to prepare him to take over leadership of the church. The people would know that when Clark left there would still be worship and Bible study. The building was only a small part of the requirements for a congregation.

At long last, spring did arrive. This time it

did not come slowly as spring so often does. One day it was still winter, and the next day spring was unmistakably in the air.

The spring birds appeared, little flowers colored the hillsides, green grass carpeted the area by the flowing spring, and Nathan ran capless and nursed a runny nose.

Missie's mind quickly switched to her planting. She pulled out all her seeds, giving special attention to the ones Clark and Marty had brought with them. Spreading the little packages all across her table, she and her father began to sort and plan. Nathan and Josiah wanted to get in on the interesting activity, and soon her carefully sorted seeds were all mixed up again. Marty shepherded the boys to the kitchen for milk and cookies, and Clark and Missie continued their garden plans.

In spite of his crutch, it was Clark who tended to the plowing of the soil. He arranged little pots for planting seedlings inside and advised Missie as to what would grow best, as well as where and when to plant them.

After the garden was started, it was time for Missie to turn to her chickens. She had spotted six hens with a desire to nest, and she carefully selected a setting of eggs for each one of them. Clark helped her with the coops, and the hens were housed in fine style. Missie placed her settings under the mothers-to-be and marked her calendar for the coming event. Marty couldn't help smiling as she watched father and daughter work together.

The date for the church building bee was set. Wagons loaded with excited families, plenty of food, and necessary tools headed for the Newtons' ranch. Cookie had to be available at home to feed the hands who were on duty with the cattle. Wong did not go, either. He was not a builder and did not feel comfortable sharing the cooking duties with several neighborhood women, so he stayed in his own kitchen and sent a big bucket of his special doughnuts to go with the morning coffee.

Juan had discovered two experienced carpenters from town who took charge of the actual construction. The neighborhood men offered their hands and skills wherever they were needed.

Within the week the church building was lifting its spire proudly toward the sky, the barren prairie and wide horizon providing a dramatic silhouette. Señora de la Rosa wept the first time she heard the bell peal, reaching across the miles and echoing from the distant hills.

The announcement of the first service in the new church brought many new faces to the congregation that day. Clark wondered, as he looked over the crowd from his place on the platform, how many were there for social reasons or idle curiosity and how many were already genuine worshipers "in spirit and in truth." Regardless of what had brought them there that day, he saw a wonderful opportunity to open the Word of God to them.

Marty sat with Missie and her family on one of the new pews, Nathan tucked in between them and Josiah snuggled on his mother's lap. *I love the smell of new wood,* thought Marty as she looked around at the families nearby and sensed their joyful anticipation. *While we've been here,* her thoughts moved on, *God has provided a doctor for their bodies' needs and a church for their spiritual needs. Thank you, Lord!*

As the Sundays continued to come and go, Clark was pleased to see quite a few of the visitors continue to come. The regular attendees made a point of keeping in contact with each new visitor to the church.

Nathan and Josiah now spent much of their time outside during the lovely spring weather. With their grandfather's help, they had planted their own small garden and checked it daily, running to their grand-mother with progress reports.

"It's growin'!" cried Nathan one day as he burst in upon Marty.

"What's growin'?" she asked innocently.

"My garden! Come see. Come see."

Marty hurried after him. Nathan fell on his knees and pointed to some small green plants just beginning to poke their heads out of the soil. Marty didn't have the heart to tell him just then that they were weeds. *Wait until some real garden begins to grow,* she told herself, *and then we'll take care of the weeds.*

But Josiah had his own way of looking after the weeds. He pulled them up to see how they were doing, then pushed them awkwardly into the ground again and pounded on their tender tops with his pudgy palm — even the hardy weeds did not survive his "tender" care.

Eventually the "real" gardens did begin to grow. Marty was not sure who was the most excited with their growing plants — the two small boys or Missie. Marty understood. She wished she were home planting her own garden. She missed it and wondered if Ellie and the boys would be taking care of it.

Marty took another horseback ride out with Missie and the boys to view the herds. Hundreds of spring calves scampered around their bawling mothers. Marty had never seen such a sight and tucked it away in her memory to report on when she and Clark returned home.

Nathan climbed down off his pony to pick wild flowers for his two favorite ladies. Marty's smile went from him to Missie, who sat on her horse with young Josiah astraddle in front of her. Missie's face was flushed, her figure gently rounding with the new life growing within her, and her hair, teased loose by the prairie wind, fanned about her. Behind her, the hills rolled on and on like a gently dipping sage-green sea. Beyond them, the mountains lifted silver peaks to play secret games with the fluffy clouds that hung low in the sky. The scene was lovely, full of life and warmth and love — a memory Marty would cherish for many years to come.

She was thankful now that Missie and Willie had come west. She was glad she and Clark had been able to visit. She was even glad for the extra time that Clark's accident had allowed them. Missie was happy here. As Marty looked at her contented daughter, she realized that Missie really belonged here. She was a gentle part of Willie's West. Marty looked about her with new appreciation for the ever-present hills and the openness — even the wind. This land spoke of freedom, of independence, and of strength. Marty was proud that her daughter was a part of it.

They rode home in silence . . . no doubt each thinking her own thoughts. Nathan cantered ahead on Spider, manfully "breaking trail" for his mother and grandmother. Josiah, his head resting against his mother, had nodded off to sleep.

Clark was waiting for them when they returned. He had spent the day putting new legs on Cookie's worktable.

"How did you and Cookie make out?" asked Missie. She and Marty knew that Clark had been looking for an opportunity for a heart-to-heart talk with Cookie about his relationship with God.

Clark shook his head. "We had a good talk — nice an' open — but Cookie is still hesitant. He says he wants to be sure he is acceptin' Jesus Christ — not Clark Davis."

"I don't understand," said Missie.

Marty thought about the statement for a moment. "I think maybe I do," she said slowly.

"Well," Clark said modestly, "Cookie says

he admires me . . . guess 'cause we both of us had a similar kind of accident. Not much to admire a man fer, but Cookie reasons a little different than some men do. Anyway, he listens to the Word as I give it Sunday by Sunday; he sees me able to make do with one leg . . . I don't know. He's got it all mixed up as to what I can do as a man and what I can do with the Lord's help. He's not sure yet where the difference lies. Cookie's right, ya know. I don't want him to be a follower of Clark Davis. Iffen he can't find the difference here, he should wait until he does. No good followin' a man. Nothin' I can give to Cookie he can't find in himself."

"Sounds strange to me," mused Missie. "I've never thought of anyone getting mixed up about who to be following before. Seems plain to me that Jesus is the only way to heaven."

"I left Cookie my Bible and marked some verses for 'im to read. I hope he can understand their meanin'."

"We're gonna have to do some praying," Missie said simply as Clark and Nathan moved away with the horses and she and Marty walked on to the house, Josiah asleep in her arms. "If Pa can't make Cookie see the difference, how will Willie or Henry ever do it?"

Eventually they learned that it was Lane who showed Cookie the difference. He walked into the cook shack and found Cookie frowning over Clark's Bible.

"I still don't figure it," mumbled Cookie.

"Don't figure what?" asked Lane, reaching for the ever-ready coffeepot.

"If I take on this here religion, will I be doin' it to try to become a man like Clark Davis?"

"What's wrong with bein' a man like Clark Davis?"

"Nothin'. Nothin' I can see. Only he says thet tryin' to be like 'im ain't gonna git me one step closer to those pearly gates yer always talkin' 'bout."

"Oh, thet," said Lane, understanding Cookie's dilemma. "He's right."

"But how can I be like *Jesus?*" asked Cookie in frustration. "I don't even *know* Him."

"Forgit 'bout bein' *like* Him fer now," said Lane. "Yer tryin' to start too far ahead of yerself." Cookie looked doubtful but let Lane continue.

"You've heard it preached an' read many times thet all men are sinners?"

"Yah," grunted Cookie.

"Are ya doubtin' ya fit in thet category?"

"Shucks, no," said Cookie. "I know myself better'n thet."

"Okay," said Lane, "thet's where ya start. Now ya know yer a sinner, an' I guess if yer wantin' to copy Davis, ya don't really want to stay one."

Cookie nodded his agreement.

"Well, how ya try to clean up yer act ain't gonna make a whole lot of difference. You'll never measure up, no matter how hard ya try. Oh, ya might even git to *act* as good as Clark Davis himself, but thet won't really impress God none. He still sees deeper than the skin.

"The Bible says thet man looks on the outside, but God looks on the heart. Also says thet the heart of man is 'desperately wicked.' But the good news is thet our hearts can be changed. Now, thet there's the startin' place.

"Jesus, holy an' pure, died fer every dirty, wicked heart thet ever beat. All we gotta do is see what we are, an' who He is, an' accept fer ourselves what He did. Thet's all there is to it. From there on, He does the workin' on makin' ya a follower."

Cookie's eyes opened wide at the simplicity of it. Lane gulped the last of his coffee, placed his cup on the table, and headed for the door.

When he reached the door he hesitated, turned to Cookie, and said softly, "All ya gotta do is ask Him."

After Lane was gone, Cookie did.

NINETEEN
PLANS AND FAREWELLS

Clark and Marty began to talk about when they should go home, talking quietly together in the privacy of the little soddy. At first it was like a dream to be thinking of boarding the slow-moving train again and leaving behind the West that they had come to respect and the family they loved so deeply. Marty wished there was a way she could bundle them all up and take them home with her. But then she thought of Willie and his love for his spread, Missie and the sun reflecting in her eyes, and Nathan and Josiah as they rushed about their beloved hills with the wind whipping at their hair. And she knew she would not want to pick them up by their roots and try to transplant them — not really.

Marty's thoughts turned more and more to her farm-home family. *How're Clare and his young Kate doing in the little log house? Is Arnie still seeing the preacher's daughter?*

What is the girl really like? Is Ellie entertaining any gentleman callers? Which of the neighborhood young men will be the first one to notice our pretty young daughter who is now a woman? She wondered if Luke still nursed his dream of going off to train as a doctor and how Dr. Watkins and the boy were getting along. Marty was anxious to get home again and have some of her questions answered.

A long letter from Ellie arrived. She told about the new grass and leaves on the flowering shrubs. She spoke of the songbirds that were back and the new colt in the pasture. She reported that Clare had plowed the garden spot and she and Kate had planted the garden — more than they would ever be using themselves, she was sure, but they just couldn't seem to stop once they had gotten started. She told of Nandry's tears of joy and sorrow upon receiving the news of her father. She wrote that Nandry had immediately sat down and penned a long letter to Clae and Joe. Ellie gave news about the neighbors, the church, and the school. But she did not say how Clare and Kate were doing in the little house, or if Arnie was still seeing the preacher's daughter, or if she, Ellie, was receiving gentleman callers, or how Luke was doing in his quest

316

of becoming a doctor. Marty's heart yearned to know all the answers.

"Clark," she said, folding up the letter for the third time, "I think it's time we got us some tickets."

Clark ran a hand over the rope he was braiding for Nathan. "Yeah," he agreed, "I think it is. We best have us a chat with Willie an' Missie tonight."

That evening Marty expected some protests when they voiced their decision. Missie put down the cup of coffee she had just poured and took a deep breath.

"No use pretending that we didn't know it had to come," she said quietly. "No use fussing about it. You must be powerful lonesome for the ones at home. I marvel that you were able to stay away this long." She poured another cup of coffee and handed it to Willie. "Of course, I wish you could just stay on here forever. But I know better. Truth is, I'm thankful for every day we've already had."

Willie cleared his throat and ran a hand through his thick hair. "Don't know as how I'm gonna git along without yer pair of hands," he said to Clark. "Can't believe the number of little things you've seen to over the winter months — things thet none of us ever seemed to find time fer."

Clark smiled. "Got a good idea," he said. "Why don't I see iffen I can talk yer pa into comin' out fer a spell? He's awful handy round a place. Never seen a man thet could make things look better in short order than yer pa. How 'bout it?"

Willie grinned. "I'd like thet," he said sincerely. "Seems like a long time since I seen my pa."

"When do you plan on going?" asked Missie.

"I'll be ridin' into town tomorra to check out the trains," returned Clark. "No use waitin' till it gits so hot one can hardly stand the ride. It was pretty uncomfortable at times fer yer ma when we came out last year. Thought it might be a little cooler iffen we go right away."

Missie was silent.

Marty looked at her daughter and caught her blinking away tears.

"We've loved having you," Missie finally managed. "You know that. I'm so sorry we have to send you back to the rest of the family different than you came, Pa. Hope they won't hold it against us and the West."

"Why should they?" asked Clark. "Accidents aren't confined to one place. Jest before we left home, a neighbor farmer got drug by a team of horses and lost *both* his legs."

"Still," said Missie, "it's going be a shock for them when they actually see you."

"I don't think any of 'em'll take it too hard," said Clark comfortably.

"We're gonna miss ya at the church," put in Willie. "Can't believe how much interest there is since we started to have real services."

"Thet won't stop," Clark answered. "Henry is all prepared to give ya Bible lessons jest as I was doin'. He'll do a fine job. I already wrote to Joe to send Henry out some good books on the Bible fer studyin'. I expect Henry to really git into 'em. He loves studyin' the Word and will bring to the people everything he can find. I think Henry is gonna make a fine lay preacher."

"We're glad for Henry," Missie said. "He's been a great help and a good friend ever since we left home."

"Ya have some very fine neighbors here," Marty said with feeling. "I'm so relieved, Missie, to know ya have ladies to visit and share with and a good doctor close by so ya won't need to go way up to Tettsford Junction fer this next little one."

"So am I," Missie agreed, reaching out to take Willie's hand. "That was what I dreaded most 'bout havin' Nathan an' Josiah — the long months of bein' away from Willie."

"Well, if I'm gonna make thet ride into town tomorra, I guess I should be gittin' to bed. Thet's a long way fer a slow rider to be travelin'." Clark stood and lifted his crutch into position.

"Would ya prefer the team to a saddle horse?" asked Willie.

"Hey, thet sounds like a good idea. Might be I'll even take young Nathan along with me, if his mother agrees."

"He'd love to go," said Missie. "He's really going to miss you. Both of you. He won't know what to do with himself when you leave."

"Won't be long until Nathan will be needin' school. I know ya have been teachin' him yerself, Missie, since ya had trainin' and some experience with schoolin.' Will ya keep on with thet?" asked Marty.

"Willie and some of the neighbor men are meeting at Juan's on Wednesday night. There are several families whose children are much older than Nathan, and they are most anxious to get them some schooling before they're so old they think they don't even *need* school. I love teaching our boys, but I think they will do well in a real school

320

with other children."

"Glad to hear thet."

"The church committee is going to tell them they can meet in the church if they want to."

"Thet's a good idea," said Clark with enthusiasm. "I sure hope it all works out fer 'em. Now, we better git. I'll be by to pick up yer son 'bout eight, if thet's all right."

"That'll be fine. He'll be up and ready to go. Why don't you both come on over and have breakfast with us first?"

"Oh no, dear, we don't want —"

"Ma," said Missie, "please. There won't be too many days for us to have a meal together. Let's make the most of the ones we have left."

Marty kissed her daughter and agreed on breakfast the next morning.

Clark and Nathan enjoyed a leisurely drive into town. Nathan, curious about everything he heard and saw, kept up an excited stream of questions and comments. Clark realized that the young boy was truly ready for school.

"What ya plannin' to be when ya grow up, boy?" asked Clark.

"I don't know, Grandpa. Some days I wanna be a rancher like my pa. An' some-

times I wanna be a foreman like Scottie, an'
some days I wanna be a cowboy like Lane,
but most of all I think I wanna be a cook
like Cookie."

Clark laughed. The ranch was really all
the life the boy knew. Clark determined to
send Nathan a packet of good books.

"What do you wanna be, Grandpa?"

"Ya mean when I grow up?"

"Yer already growed."

"Oh yah," said Clark, "guess I am at that."

"What ya gonna be?" asked Nathan again.

"Well," said Clark, "I'm a farmer."

"What do farmers do?"

"Much like a rancher, only they don't
raise quite so many cows and horses. An'
they might have pigs or sheep or even goats
to go with them other animals. An' they
plow fields, an' pick rock, an' pull stumps,
an' plant grain thet they harvest every fall.
Then they build haystacks and store feed
fer their animals to eat in the winter months.
And they butcher an' cure meat, an' chop
wood, an' doctor sick critters, an' take in
garden vegetables, an' fix fences."

"Boy," said Nathan, "farmers do lotsa
stuff, huh, Grandpa?"

"Guess that's right."

"Can ya do all thet, Grandpa?"

"Shore. Don't take nobody special to do

all thet."

"Boy, ya can do lots of things with only one leg, can't ya, Grandpa?"

"Well, ya see, son, when I was doin' all those things I still had me two legs. So I been thinkin' some lately of how I can still do the same things. It's gonna take some special tools. Ya know the piece of harness I made fer myself so I could balance and still handle the horse an' the plow?"

Nathan nodded and smiled. "That's kind of a funny contraption, Grandpa," he commented, and they both shared a chuckle.

"Well, I plan on makin' a lot of things like thet," Clark explained. "I couldn't start to work on them yet, 'cause they've got to be measured jest so, to fit the different things I'll be usin' — like the plow an' the rake an' the seeder. I'm gonna make 'em all when I git home. I got this here idea of how I'll fix the plow, see . . ." And Clark commenced to tell Nathan all the details of his idea while the little boy's eyes opened wide as he listened. The miles melted away as the two worked together on Clark's plans.

In town Clark discovered that the next available eastbound train was leaving the following Tuesday. He bought their tickets and then took Nathan to the general store for a treat. They also pocketed some sweets for Josiah, then headed the team for home.

The news of the upcoming departure had Marty in a flurry of plans and activities. She was sure she had much to do to prepare for the journey, but when she set about to begin, she found it wasn't much after all — not nearly what it had been in preparing for their trip west. Now there was only their own luggage to pack, since all the things they had brought with them for Missie and the family would be staying right there. Marty relaxed and enjoyed her last days, spending as much time with the boys as she could.

She cleaned up the tiny soddy and bade it a fond farewell, then moved their things back into Missie's fine house for the remaining days.

That evening Willie came home from the de la Rosas' with exciting news. The community had voted to begin the new school in the church building. Henry's Melinda had been asked to teach. Her close neighbor, Mrs. Netherton, an older woman with no children, had agreed to stay with Melinda's young son while she was at school. Since Melinda was reluctant to leave her boy too long, the first year of school would be held only for three days a week. Still, the neighborhood agreed that this arrangement was far better than no school at all.

Willie and Missie had decided that Nathan would be allowed to join the school-bound crowd. Since Melinda would be driving right by their ranch, she had agreed to pick up the young scholar.

As each final day together ticked by, Marty took special note. A little clock ran in her mind: *This is our last Friday . . . our last Saturday . . . our last service in the little church.* That Sunday she prepared for the service with extra care. Clark had already shared with her some of his thoughts on the Scripture portion for the day. Marty felt them to be most appropriate on their last day with this congregation they had learned to love. There was no better message that Clark could leave with them.

When Clark stood before the group on that last Sunday, he read solemnly, yet exultantly, from Jeremiah 9:23 and 24: "Thus saith the Lord, Let not the wise man glory in his wisdom, neither let the mighty man glory in his might, let not the rich man glory in his riches: but let him that glorieth glory in this, that he understandeth and knoweth me, that I am the Lord which exercise lovingkindness, judgment, and righteousness, in the earth: for in these things I delight, saith the Lord." As she listened, Marty prayed for the individuals who sat in the seats around her. Her desire, as well as Clark's, was that each one of them might deeply understand and live the truth of the Scriptures, and this one in particular.

After the service had ended, Clark invited Henry to speak to the congregation. It was commonly known that when Clark left, Henry would take up the reins of leadership.

With emotion in his voice, Henry expressed his thanks to Clark and Marty for their guidance and encouragement over the months they had been with them, the congregation echoing his appreciation with amens and yeses. Then Clark and Marty, taken completely by surprise, were guests of honor as the whole fellowship gathered around to give them a farewell celebration. Food was spread out on makeshift tables, and the women served the group, then joined the men and children digging in with relish.

Underlying the festivities and laughter was a feeling of sadness since in just two days the Davises would be leaving them. Clark and Marty appreciated each one who came with a special thank-you shining in his or her eyes and warm handshakes and embraces. They were special, these people.

They were special because they were Christian brothers and sisters. Clark and Marty were sure they would miss them — not family by blood but by adoption into the family of God.

TWENTY
HOMEWARD BOUND

When Tuesday morning arrived, Marty was packed and ready to go. As Willie brought the team around and Missie prepared her sons for the trip to town, Clark went to say a last farewell to the ranch hands, and Marty slipped out of the house and made one last trip to the little soddy. She was not as nostalgic about it for her own sake as for Missie's. Marty had spent a winter in the soddy by choice. Missie had made it a home because it was all that was available to her.

Marty stood and gazed around the little room once again. In her fancy she could see Missie as a very young bride bending over the tiny stove with its cow-chip fire, preparing the evening meal. In the cradle at the end of the bed would rest their tiny baby, Nathan. Willie would return from his long, hard day of herding cattle to be greeted with love and concern and a simple meal.

Marty could picture, too, the growing

Nathan, the Christmas gathering of ranch hands, the visits with new neighbors. Marty would cherish her own mental images of the little soddy. Her own time spent there helped her to more clearly picture Missie in it.

Yes, she and Clark had been happy in the soddy, too. Those long evenings as she sat sewing and Clark pored over his Bible, sharing with her special truths as he found them and inviting her thoughts on particular verses — these were memories to treasure. Perhaps it would be many weeks before she and Clark would have so many hours of each day to cherish as their own without interruption from the daily demands of farm and family.

Marty slowly retraced her steps to the house — Missie's beautiful home. Marty had never seen a home that was more comfortable or more tastefully furnished. She was proud of Missie and her homemaking abilities.

Marty rounded the corner to find they were loading the wagon. She stepped forward to take her place. All the ranch hands who were not on duty were there to shake her hand, and Marty spoke to each of them. Cookie was the last in the line.

The old ranch cook stepped forward, his

hand outstretched.

"Cookie," said Marty, emotion choking her voice, "we are so thankful to God fer yer choosin' to follow Him. Yer jest special to us in so many ways."

Cookie changed his mind and gave Marty an affectionate hug instead.

Lane moved forward and took Clark's hand. He said nothing, but his eyes said what he could not put into words.

Just as the wagon was about to move out of the yard, Wong came running, waving a bundle in his hands. Some fresh doughnuts, a treat for the trip, he said. Marty and Clark thanked him warmly, and he beamed as he bobbed his head.

"Much thanks," he said. "Much thanks for special joy you brought this house and to Wong's kitchen. Come again, maybe?"

The wagon pulled away amid hat waving and calls, and then they were on their way.

Marty's view was blurred with tears as she looked back from the hillside where she'd had her first look at Missie's home. So much had happened there to endear so many people to her heart.

Josiah climbed on her lap, and she held him close all the way to town. Nathan chattered excitedly, voicing his perspective that Grandma and Grandpa were privileged indeed to be passengers on a real moving train.

"An' someday I'm gonna come all the way on the train to the farm an' see ya," he promised fervently.

And Josiah echoed, "See ya."

"Yeah," said Nathan, "me and Joey. We'll come an' see ya."

"That would be most wonderful," said Marty and held her Joey even closer.

When they reached the town, Clark checked their trunk through, and they gathered their hand baggage and went to get a cup of coffee while they waited for the train.

It was hard to know what should be said in their last few minutes together. It seemed like there was still so much left to be said, in spite of the fact they had spent all these months talking.

They filled the time with small talk and reminders of messages for each one of the family on the farm.

It was nearly time to get back to the station when Scottie appeared.

"I wasn't able to see ya off at the house," he said, extending his hand to Clark, "but I shore didn't want to miss sayin' goodbye. Guess I needn't say thet we're gonna miss ya round the spread. S'pose now I'll have to mend my own halters and clean my own barns."

Clark smiled. He didn't feel he had helped Scottie out that much, but he knew what he had done had been appreciated. He shook Scottie's hand firmly. "Ya'll always have a warm spot in our hearts an' prayers," he told the ranch foreman, and Scottie smiled.

They walked slowly to the train station. Already the train was sending up great puffs of smoke as the firebox was filled in preparation for the departure. Long cars were filled with bawling steers, and Marty knew they would share the ride with many cattle heading for market. She wondered if some of Willie's herd might even be on board.

It was time for the last tearful good-bye.

"Pa," said Missie, her voice choked, "do you think you could ship out some apple cuttings by train? I've been missing those trees an awful lot."

Clark was thoughtful, not sure that apple trees would grow in the area, but he nodded his head. "Why not?" he said. "It's shore worth a try. Ya can plant them down by yer spring an' make sure they git plenty of water. Might not produce too much fruit, but ya might git enough fer a pie or two."

Missie laughed through her tears. "Truth is," she stated, "I won't even care too much if I don't get fruit. It's the blossoms I miss the most. It seems to me they promise spring, and love, and happiness every time they appear."

Clark gave his daughter a long understanding hug.

They all embraced one last time and told one another again how much the visit had meant to each of them. Marty and Clark held their two grandsons for as long as they dared, and then the "all aboard" was called and they waved one last time and climbed onto the train.

Marty waved until the train turned a curve and the town and her family were left behind. She wiped her tears on her handkerchief and resolved that she would cry no more.

The traveling days moved by, measured by the rhythms of the steel wheels. Each revolution took them farther away from Willie and Missie but closer to the other members of their family.

Marty didn't find the return trip quite so difficult, nor so uncomfortably warm. Maybe now she knew what to expect and set her mind accordingly.

There were a few stops at small towns here and there — some taking far too long

— but then they traveled on again, day and night. On the third day, they pulled into the town where they had switched trains on their westward journey. Again it meant an overnight stay. Clark and Marty both remembered the dirty little hotel and its bedbugs.

"Surely we can do better than thet," Clark assured Marty and made some discreet inquiries. They were pointed to the home of an elderly lady who, they were told, kept roomers on occasion. Fortunately, the woman had a vacancy and accepted them as overnight guests.

By the time they made their way back to the station the next morning, shoppers were beginning to appear on the streets. The town was again awakening as it had done the year before.

When they reached the train station, Clark held the door for Marty and she passed through and headed for some seats near the window. She would sit and wait while Clark checked out the departure time.

Clark walked closely behind her to settle the luggage he carried down beside her before going over to the ticket counter. Other passengers milled about the room.

Marty heard the loud voice of a youngster. "Ma, look — look at thet poor man."

Marty's head came up slowly and she looked around, wondering who the unfortunate person might be. She spotted no one who fit the description.

"Ya lookin' fer the man?"

At the sound of Clark's voice, Marty flushed, embarrassed to be caught staring about out of curiosity. Her eyes admitted to Clark that she had indeed been looking for "the poor man."

Clark was quick to ease her guilt. "I was, too," he confessed. "Did ya spot 'im?"

Marty shook her head.

"Me neither," said Clark and then began to chuckle.

Marty looked at him in surprise.

"Thet is," went on Clark, "till I looked at myself."

"Yerself?"

Clark chuckled again.

"He was talkin' 'bout *me*, Marty."

"You?"

Then Marty's gaze fell to the pinned-up empty pant leg and the crutch in Clark's hand. Her breath caught in a little gasp. It was true. The boy was speaking of Clark — and "the poor man" was chuckling!

Then Marty saw it — the humor of it, the glory of it. They both had completely forgotten that Clark was considered handicapped

— "the poor man." They reached for each other and laughed together till tears of joy ran freely down their faces.

ABOUT THE AUTHOR

Janette Oke was born in Champion, Alberta, to a Canadian prairie farmer and his wife, and she grew up in a large family full of laughter and love. She is a graduate of Mountain View Bible College in Alberta, where she met her husband, Edward, and they were married in May of 1957. After pastoring churches in Indiana and Canada, the Okes spent some years in Didsbury and Calgary, where Edward served in several positions on college faculties while Janette continued her writing. She has written over five dozen novels for adults and children, and her book sales total over twenty-two million copies.

The Okes have three sons and one daughter, all married, and are enjoying their dozen grandchildren. Edward and Janette are active in their local church and make their home near Didsbury, Alberta.

Visit Janette Oke's Web site at:
www.janetteoke.com.